"I appreciated the kinds lar, little-discussed aspect of an important and neglected t , so in a sensitive and appealing fashion. I found the reading of it very interesting. You enable the reader to feel as if he/she were really there with Tim. The persons in the story come across as real people. The sincerity of what you write is one of the most appealing features of the book. The writing flows smoothly."

*Millard J. Erickson, Ph.D.*
*Vice President and Dean of Theology*
*Bethel Theological Seminary, St. Paul, Minn.*

"Your presentation affected each one of us very deeply. Our profound thanks for being willing to enter into your own pain again, in celebration of Tim's life. Your story, your courage in telling it, and your absolute fearlessness enable us to alter our perceptions and begin a change in heart."

*Harvey County (Kansas) Hospice, Inc.*

"This woman is wonderful, courageous; learned a lot; entire school should hear her; very moving, excellent; very inspirational; helped to make one understand homosexuals are okay; very helpful, informative — good to know parent's viewpoint."

*Bethany College (Kansas)*
*Helping Profession Seminar*

"Beverly Barbo's The Walking Wounded is a gentle, sensitive, loving response of a family as they experienced this sorrow which is like no other sorrow. Revealing strong personal faith and dignity, this family literally walked through their son's last year with a quiet triumph over whatever negativism they might have encountered because they knew the special qualities of this very special son. I want to say thank you to Beverly for making the struggle so real without the burden of technical medical information that is so prevalent in many writings about AIDS. Her spiritual equilibrium shines through as she walks through these deep waters.

*Elinor Kirby Lewallen, President*
*Federation of Parents and Friends*
*of Lesbians and Gays, Inc.*

"This is a wonderful, heartwarming, and spiritually strengthening testimonial. Tim is at peace, and you make it abundantly clear that you and Dave, as well as your family, are also at peace with yourselves and God."

*Elston Flohr, Ph.D.*
*Professor Emeritus of English*
*Bethany College, Lindsborg, Kansas*

"It is devastating and heartbreaking – an experience!"

*Denver*

"This is a book that should be available in every library."

*Missouri*

ii

"This book will help people see the truth and only the truth can set us free."

*Kansas City*

"We received your book – have read it and re-read it. Needless to say, we cried, laughed an cried some more. So many of our friends want to read the book. It will be dog-eared in no time."

*Los Angeles*

"Mrs. Barbo is a very special lady. Tim was a lucky son to have her for his mom. She made one realize that gay people are real people too."

*Solomon Valley (Kansas) Hospice*

"I intend to pass it along to my family and then to many others in the community whom I'm sure will be comforted, impressed and inspired as I. I know there will be many requests for copies. It is one of the most sensitive and explicit expressions of understanding I have ever encountered."

*Los Angeles*

"As Christmas comes, I want you to know my life has deepened since the last one. Hearing you share, along with reading your book has caused me to take a second look at the homosexual condition. It has added a new dimension to our 'loving one another' and I want to thank you for helping me open this door."

*Jo Larson*
*Lutheran Pastor*
*Kansas*

"Our profound thanks for being willing to enter into your own pain again, in celebration of Tim's life. Your story, your courage in telling it and your absolute fearlessness enables us to alter our perceptions and begin a change of heart."

*Carole Hull, M.A.*
*Executive Director*
*Harvey County Hospice, Kansas*

# The Walking Wounded

A mother's true story of her son's homosexuality
and his eventual AIDS-related death!

**CARLSONS' Publishing**
P.O. Box 364
Lindsborg, Kansas

## The Walking Wounded

First Printing 1987
Second Printing 1989
Copyright (c) 1987 by Beverly Barbo

Published in the United States of America by CARLSONS', P.O. Box 364, Lindsborg, Kansas.

Printed in the United States of America by BARBOS', 114 S. Main, Suite B, Lindsborg, Kansas.

Library of Congress Catalog Card Number: 87-72944

ISBN 0-944996-01-9

# THE WALKING WOUNDED

## TABLE OF CONTENTS

*Dedicated to Tim, who lived his life with a fierce inner strength and faced death with faith and courage.*

## ACKNOWLEDGEMENT

To my husband, who enabled me to be with Tim throughout the last year of his life: Dave, thank you for the time you spent and the tears you shed as you transferred this story from my handwritten notes to the word processor. It couldn't have been done without your love and support.

To Tom, a cherished friend, whom I love as a son: I will always remember how easy it has been for us to laugh and cry together. Thank you for your wonderful love and care for Tim.

To my family and Tom's family, who showed Tim and Tom what love and acceptance are all about.

To all those who, in their support and love, were open and willing to share their lives.

I love you all.

Sadly, to protect people in this homophobic society, I have had to change some names and locations. There were many pictures that could not be included because of "guilt" by association. On our family picture, which is my treasure and had to be included, Tom's face is faded back. I truly hope and pray that someday this will not be necessary.

# TIM'S LIFE IN PICTURES

# PREFACE

There are many wounded souls in our society today, most walking around, functioning, and not acknowledging to others just how deep the wound is.

In this book I will focus on the segment of society that is the target of many slings and arrows, and that can find shelter in few places, not even the church. My son, Tim, was a homosexual who made his life in this particular community of the walking wounded.

Christ said, "Come to me, all who labor and are heavy laden, and I will give you rest" (Matthew 11:28). If anyone is heavy ladened and burdened, it is the homosexual. Society in general, as well as the church, has heaped mountains of reproach and hate upon these people because of misconceptions, misunderstanding, fear and ages of prejudice.

"Come now, let us reason together" (Isaiah 1:18) is all that I am asking and perhaps we may lighten one another's burdens.

There is a story about the birds and how they viewed their wings as burdens until they learned how to use them. When they accepted them as being good, they learned how to fly and delighted in how free they could be. Many gay people don't want to acknowledge their homosexuality because it truly is a burden in our society today. They are forced to choose the prison of living a lie to be acceptable, rather than admit to who and what they are, thereby being rejected and heavily laden with the reproach of others. Perhaps if we could begin by simply accepting each other as we are, that healing could begin and all of us, all of the walking wounded, including the homosexual, could be free indeed.

"Even though I walk through the valley of the shadow of death, I fear no evil; for thou art with me" (Psalm 23:4). Our family, along with Tim's life partner, Tom, have been wandering through the valley for a long time. We lost Tim along the way because he was mortally wounded. We simply took different paths out of the valley. Tim went into the very presence of God while the rest of us are still struggling, trying to find some meaning in our long journey and personal loss.

This book is not a highly researched study, neither is it a theological treatise. It is a collection of little everyday happenings which are a part of the whole fabric of Tim's story.

It is a mother's feelings about how our family functioned in a time of great stress.

It is a tribute to the love between two young men, and the selfless care and devotion Tom demonstrated to Tim.

It is Tim's story as seen through his mother's eyes.

It is about a young man's life and what it was like for him to grow up gay and to live and die in a homophobic world.

It is a call for understanding and care.

*Beverly Barbo*

Family, Milwaukee, Early 1960's

Family, Denver, Early 1979

# ONE

# Outside The Narrow Gates

## October 1986

My son is supposed to die tonight. I can do nothing about it, only be here and love him.

Why is my son dying? Because he made some bad choices a few years ago, one of which resulted in the disease AIDS, and the AIDS-related cancer, Kaposi Sarcoma, is now killing him. It has been killing him for many months now, and maybe tonight my Timothy will find sweet release. The carnage this disease visits upon the body is unthinkable and the pain is intense. Everyone is helpless against it from the beginning. There are sometimes small victories, but the war is always lost.

Is God helpless against this plague? Where is the all-loving God now when Tim and I need Him the most? Is He too busy with something else? I think not, because it has to be some higher power that is keeping me together. The nurses and doctors tell me that I am holding up very well, and it can't be simply strength of character. Oh, I could rail against God and deny Him, but that would not make Him any less real. If I would say I cannot believe, would that make Him cease to exist?

I have often thought that people write books not only as a catharsis for their most personal feelings but also to try to explain God. Perhaps that is what I am doing.

Over the past few years and the last few months particularly, I have had to change my perceptions of God to accommodate the circumstances of my life. I have had to scream and kick my way out of the comfortable little box I had been living in and deal with things as they are, not as I wished them to be.

Up until twelve years ago you could have called us the model middle class American family. We lived very comfortably in a split level house in a lovely Denver suburb. My husband, Dave, had a good job with a steady income; our children, Pam and Mike, were doing well, and with a few exceptions our youngest, Tim, was all right. I knew that Tim was not readily accepted by others and that he wasn't particularly happy. I also knew that he was very different from Pam and Mike and had some deep unresolved pain, but I had prayed about that and it didn't seem as if there was anything more to do but to leave him in the hands of God. My greatest fear, that my son was gay, was something I kept in the deepest recesses of my heart. We were devout Christians ... and the Bible, as I understood it, said "it is an abomination" (Lev. 18:22 and 20:13), and I couldn't believe God would allow that in our lives.

It was at that time that I felt the "church" was not enough, that my prayers were being ignored and that life was passing by without my being a real participant in it. What good was I doing? Was I making any difference to anyone in this world?

God had never audibly spoken to me and I know He had never written in the dust on my coffee table. Was I not praying worthily, whatever that means, or was there some specific sin in my life that I had not confessed? To my knowledge there was no reason why there should be an obstacle to my communications with the Almighty. Through all of these years my family had tried to be part of God's kingdom on earth. The knowledge that we were sinners and imperfect had been acknowledged by each one of us, and the fact that we needed Christ as our Saviour and Intercessor was real to us. So upon confession of faith, each of us had been baptized into the "Body of Christ". As I look back I now realize that we had no idea of what that meant, but it was a good feeling to be an integral part of the congregation.

One day as I was making the beds there seemed to be such an emptiness inside me that I began to weep. In my frustration I punched the pillows and cried out saying, "God, there has to be more to the Christian life than this!" There was the usual profound silence at the time, but from the events that followed I know He must have said, "OK, Beverly, we will see where your source really is!"

Had I been able to see into the future I am sure that in my "humanness" I would have begged to stay in my comfortable little box.

It had been so easy to live in the narrow confines where I accepted and acted on standards which required thoughtless obedience. God permitted circumstances

3

which were to throw my neat little world into chaos. I fully realize that trouble is not unique to me; however, I will tell you that in the months following my foolish outburst Dave lost his job, so I had to look for full time employment; my mother-in-law moved in with us; my father had brain surgery which caused irreparable damage; I had to have a lump in my breast biopsied (fortunately it was benign); and after attempted suicide, Tim came out of the closet.

When I would wake up in the morning, I would ask God, "What do you have for me today? I can hardly wait."

Perhaps it would have been easier to retreat to a world of right and wrong, black and white as interpreted by the church, but then what would I have done with my homosexual son? I was not ready to sentence him to hell for what he was. The circumstances forced me to study and try to interpret the possibilities of this critical issue, and I found the answer not in black and white, but in shades of gray. After all, Tim was the same person after the revelation that he was before and I loved him. Was he not family, or not Christian, just because he was gay?

With an integration of faith and learning, the conclusions I arrived at were not always consistent with strict fundamentalism. I had to transcend what I had believed for years to be a divinely ordained rule and examine all of the possibilities within a Christian context. There was terror and conflict as I struggled to open my mind, soul and spirit to new thought because I didn't know where the road might lead, and it was uncomfortable wandering too far from the familiar.

Dave and I fought the battle together as we searched for the leading of the Spirit to discern what Christianity

4

was all about and what Jesus meant to all creation, including the homosexual.

Tim's situation was devastating to us, for even though I had suspected it for so long, as long as it wasn't said, it wasn't so. After the initial shock and my resolve to do anything possible to fix it, sad as it was to say, my first thought was, "What will the people at church think?"

The desperate concern about the opinions of others can bring about deafness to God's voice when that voice directs the questioning of one's own belief system which has been molded and reinforced by society and the congregation functioning as the church. I found the possibility that society and the church condemns when God does not.

Throughout the painful tearing-away process, my husband and I got a new perspective on what it meant to be a Christian and responsible to God and man. Very simply it seemed to come down to this:

*"You shall love the Lord your God with all your heart, and with all your soul, and with all your mind, and all your strength.' The second is this, 'You shall love your neighbor as yourself.' There is no other commandment greater than these"* (Mark 12:30-31).

We are also commanded to "love our neighbor" in Matthew 19:19, Lev. 19:18, Luke 10:27, Romans 13:9, Galatians 5:14 and James 2:8, to "love one another" in John 15:12 and John 15:17. Finally in Micah 6:8, we read, "He has showed you, O man, what is good; and what does the Lord require of you but to do justice, and to love kindness, and to walk humbly with your God?"

Homosexuality is a fact of life. From the literature that I have read, homosexuals have always seemed to comprise 5-10% of the population. If this is true, consider who is around the next time a "fag" joke is told or when the homosexual is condemned from the pulpit. Is it the gay man or the lesbian woman, is it their mother or father, sister or brother, aunts, uncles or cousins? How many people are sitting in the church pews pretending it doesn't apply to them but are being destroyed inside thinking that they or a loved one is unacceptable to God? There is a hidden minority in most churches, and if the statistics are correct, all people are touched in some way; they just don't know it.

Society in general and the church in particular seem to think of homosexuals in terms of another species—those people who are depraved, sick and sinful and must be kept at a distance. Homosexuals are further depersonalized because society never thinks of homosexuality in terms of love, only sexual activity and lust.

Though some people may have a choice, I know others do not. Would people freely choose a lifestyle by which they would be called immoral and have fire and damnation called down upon them by the church? Would they choose to be called sick and perverted by society? Would they choose to be called illegal by the law? Would they choose to be disowned and thrown out by their parents? I believe any thinking person would agree that to chance facing all of the rejection, homosexuality has to involve more than choice.

My son, Tim, had no more choice about his homosexuality than he had about having blond hair and blue eyes.

He was a constitutional homosexual, which means exclusive in his sexual orientation.

Choices enter in only when one decides whether to accept oneself as a homosexual and then what to do with this sexuality. It is the same for all people, homosexual and heterosexual, as to what behavioral and moral standards are observed and what responsibility is taken. All people should develop a responsible ethic for their lives.

Homosexuals have no support systems within society or the church, even when they enter into a life long commitment with someone they love. Rather, with the stresses put on the relation ship by the straight community it is more likely to fall apart. Therefore, the gay community has to be its own support group, and I have seen the strength of that community in this time of death and dying. There are those who condemn the gay church because they cannot be reconciled to the concept of a Christian homosexual, but I ask the question, "Would my son and his partner have been welcome in your congregation?"

Society declares the homosexual an immoral deviate and demands the impossible, that is to change, to be normal, that is to become heterosexual. (Freud said to change a homosexual orientation into heterosexual is not much more promising than to do the reverse.)[1] Also the requirement of acceptability put forth by some denominations, that the gay person live a totally celibate life, which according to scripture is a "special gift" to only a few (Math. 19:10-12, I Cor. 7:7), is indeed an unwarranted cruelty to put on the shoulders of someone who may already be confused about who he is or why he is.

The concept some have is that if a homosexual will turn to God and/or accept Christ as Saviour and Lord of his life, he will be cured and miraculously be rid of that curse forever. All of my children were brought up in the church and were taught the reality of God and Christ's death as a propitiation for our sin. The Spirit spoke to each one individually and each one made a confession and commitment.

Pam and Mike were acceptable Christians, according to church doctrine, but Tim could not claim that because of the general interpretation of certain scriptures. No matter how he prayed that God would intervene, it never happened and he was still a homosexual with all the excess baggage of guilt that goes with it.

One gay man wrote that if God truly hates the homosexual, He must also hate the homosexual Christian. This would appear to be an unreconcilable dilemma. Because of his love for God he is promised that God loves and accepts him, yet on the other hand he is taught that God hates homosexuals, and that is what he is.

Malcolm Boyd has written of this irony in **"Am I Running With You, God?"**

> *They stand inside your church, Lord, and know a wholeness that can benefit it. Long ago they learned that they must regard the lilies of the field, putting their trust in you.*
>
> *Pressured to hide their identities and gifts, they have served you with an unyielding, fierce love inside the same church that condemned them.*
>
> *Taught that they must feel self-loathing, nevertheless*

*they learned integrity and dignity, and how to look into your face and laugh with grateful joy, Lord.*

*Victims of a long and continuing torture, they asserted a stubborn faith in the justice of your kingdom.*

*Negativism was drummed into them as thoroughly as if they were sheet metal. They learned what it is to be hated. Yet, despite real rejection, they insisted on attesting to the fullness and beauty of all human creation, including theirs, in your image.*

*They are alive and well and standing inside your church. Bless them, Lord, to your service.*[2]

Many marry in the hope that it will somehow, miraculously, make them normal. What usually happens is that nothing really changes and the natural same-sex urge returns (for this is normal and natural for the homosexual), and they find they can no longer live the lie. This has hurt and destroyed many families, and it is even worse when children are involved. So the gay person is further damaged in that he looks at himself as less than a whole person because of another failure in his life, even when he had tried so hard to be what he "should be."

I will not argue theology. I will only speak from my experience. What the Bible says is open to further thought and interpretation; therefore I believe people should be open to considering different spiritual points of view. Jesus never mentioned the subject of homosexuality. In the book **"Is The Homosexual My Neighbor"** (Harper & Row, 1980), Letha Scanzoni and Virginia Ramey Mollenkott have with love and consideration communicated some alternative Christian thought based on research and study all done in light of scripture. This book also offers research findings from psychological and sociological points of view as well as a wealth of sources for further study.

People speaking with a surety that they know the truth from God, often refer to the homosexual in terms of hatred and loathing because they have accepted some generalizations about the homosexual that they feel is the truth. What is truth? We all have our perceptions of truth molded by what we are taught, what we read, our life experiences, and the way we think things should be, the ideal. One person's truth may not be truth to another's concept of truth and neither may have any connection with the real truth. The truth, or what we each believe is truth can also be interpreted in shades of gray, not in absolutes. Before we condemn the homosexual (or any other group or person) because of our own personal truth, it would be wise to heed the admonition against bearing false witness.

Scripture has much to say on the dangers and cruelty of the tongue and relatively little about homosexuality, yet so many view homosexuality as the ultimate sin and an excuse "to cast out the speck in our brother's eye while ignoring the log in our own." To be responsible is to know people as a creation of God and to trust them accordingly. Negative remarks and gossip have been a tool for causing a great amount of pain to those we generalize about. Although this occurs in all minority groups, because of the context in which I am writing this refers here to the spread of homophobia.

There has never been any absolute conclusion reached on what causes homosexuality. I have done a great deal of reading on homosexuality and have found my own school of thought, generalizing from what I have read, observed and experienced.

The homosexual condition was for a long period of time considered an illness by the medical/psychological professions. Possible causes have run a gamut including: strong, aggressive, mother; abusive, cold and rejecting father; an arrested state of development; an unnatural attachment to the same-sex parent, failure to identify with the same-sex parent; over-identification with the opposite-sex parent; castration anxiety among males; narcissism; adult seduction by same sex; and the list goes on.

Parents seem to have been the people blamed most often for their children's "unnatural tendencies." If this were true, why would Dave and I have a feminine Pam, a masculine Mike, and a gay Tim?

Most of these theories have been proven false or have never been proven to be consistent, thereby necessitating new theories.

I have read about studies that prove there is a wide range of sexuality, from the totally heterosexual individual to the totally homosexual person, with people at many stages in between. This is also apparent as one becomes aware of sexual orientation and observes people and their behavior.

It seems rather obvious why homosexuality was at one time considered a mental illness. Healthy people do not go to doctors, psychologists and psychiatrists; only those with problems do, so all of the gay people the doctors saw were the maladjusted. They didn't know about the homosexuals who had accepted themselves, were successful and living quiet, responsible constructive lives.

Homosexuality is no longer considered an illness, but there seems to be more consideration that the disposition toward sexual orientation is inborn and that sex hormones play a key role. Genetics could possibly be involved as in other aberrations from what we consider the norm. Also in my experience, I have found more than one homosexual within extended families, not necessarily brothers and sisters, but cousins, aunts, uncles, etc.

After all the theories have been explored and there are no answers to the question of how and why the homosexual is, perhaps we should say, "So What?" These people are very human and like the heterosexual in every way but one—sexual orientation. Is it really important, should it make any difference?

As I observe people in the straight community I find most have no awareness of how many homosexuals they know. Yet if the secret that the gay people have would come out, they probably would be treated very differently by those they have considered as friends.

The average gay person whom I know is involved in a long- term loving relationship. He gets up in the morning, has his coffee and gets ready for work. Often in a white collar profession, he has the same stresses and responsibilities as his coworkers who happen to be straight. After work he will be found fighting the traffic to get home, fix dinner, eat, clean up the kitchen and maybe will have time to watch a little television before bed. On Saturday morning it is house cleaning and grocery shopping time. The afternoon will probably be spent tending the lawn and flowers. In the evening perhaps the couple will have friends over, or be invited to someone else's home, party a little or just go out for a quiet dinner together. Sundays may or may not include church attendance, and after dinner maybe a drive or a long walk is in order. Many times a video tape will be rented and a few other friends will come over to enjoy the movie and perhaps a barbecue later. Nothing very exciting and nothing unusual, just the ordinary couple next door.

If I give some examples of what some of my gay friends do for a living, you may have something to relate to. My son, Tim, was an account executive for Pacific Telesis; his partner, Tom, is an office manager for a large brokerage house. Jeff is an assistant Vice President of one of the largest banking chains in the country. Everett is also in the upper echelon of a large bank, while John is manager of an exclusive retail establishment just off Rodeo Drive in Hollywood. Don is an engineer. Others I personally know include a social worker, chef, many R.N.'s, doctors, artists, church workers, an entrepreneur working in real estate and oil, teachers, an advertising executive, a graphic designer, florists, hairdressers, people in management of various businesses, clergy, professional musicians, handy persons, waiters and students.

They are simply ordinary run-of-the-mill people who seem to have a flair of creativity and also an extra dose of compassion.

Brian McNaught has put out a video tape called **"On Being Gay."**[3] On it he challenges the viewers to reverse the dynamics of the social structure and think of the world as predominately gay. Homosexuality is the norm. The judges, police, teachers, priests, ministers, business people, doctors, are all gay, and oh yes, you are being brought up in a gay family.

As you grow up you hear about "those people." They are whispered about and referred to as "the breeders" and you know that whatever "breeder" means, it is not a good thing to be. You don't understand what makes them bad.

You know you are different because you don't have the same feelings about the same sex as your brothers do—you are attracted to the opposite sex. "It can't be true, I can't be a breeder because I am a good person. If I tell anyone how I feel they will not love me, and I need to be loved too."

"Maybe if I pray to God, he will change me and then it will be O.K." You pray but it doesn't happen, so the secret is carried and the self-hatred eats away at your soul and self esteem. Finally the fact of being a breeder is accepted and you have to find another breeder because you can't live without any love and affection in your life. Everyone has to belong somewhere.

While participating in this exercise one can see a glimmer of what being gay in this society really means. It is discomfiting and fearful, yet it provides insight into the lives and feelings of those that society and many churches will not acknowledge as accepted or loved by God.

So where do we go from here and what will our response be to that person who is suspected of being gay and is therefore ignored and isolated and sometimes joked about? It could even be someone that no one suspects, perhaps a policeman, athlete, secretary, or just the nice lady who lives down the street. It could be one of your best friends or even part of your family. What will you do?

A solution to this problem is up to individuals coming together as a compassionate whole, accepting in love people who have been considered the unlovely. Consider carefully as it will involve commitment. In Matthew 25:34-40 we read:

> *"Then the King will say to those at his right hand, 'Come, O blessed of my Father, inherit the kingdom prepared for you from the foundation of the world; for I was hungry and you gave me food, I was thirsty and you gave me drink, I was a stranger and you welcomed me, I was naked and you clothed me, I was sick and you visited me, I was in prison and you came to me.' Then the righteous will answer him, 'Lord, when did we see thee hungry and feed thee, or thirsty and give thee drink? And when did we see thee a stranger and welcome thee, or naked and cloth thee? And when did we see thee sick or in prison and visit thee?' And the King will answer them, 'Truly, I say to you, as you did it to one of the least of these my brethren you did it to me.'"*

My son was one of the least of these.

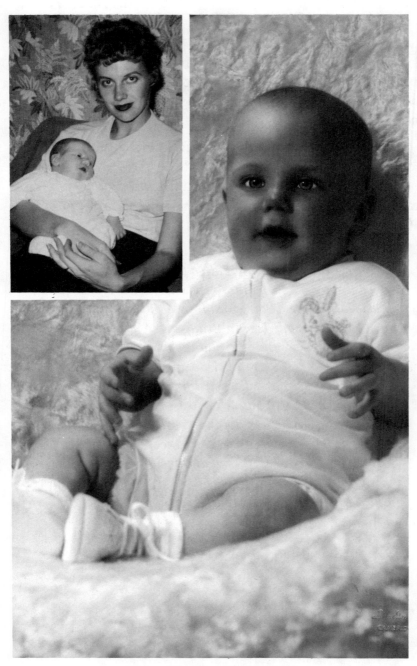

**Baby Tim (and Mother)**

# TWO

# Imminent End

## At Sherman Oaks Hospital, October 25, 1986

My son is supposed to die tonight. Dr. Knight told me that the time has finally come, that the battle is nearly over and Tim will probably not live to see the morning. My feelings are so muddled. I am glad that Tim's suffering will be over, and yet I want to hold him tight and fight off the power of death. I don't want him to leave me.

I have to ask God, "Is this the way it is meant to be?" He is so young and has so much to offer. He is flesh of my flesh and bone of my bone. I have experienced the pain and joy of his birth. I have felt the pain and pleasure of his life and am now part of the sweetness and pain of his death. We are alone in this hospital room, Tim and I.

The nurses have helped him into the hospital gown, tucked him in and connected him to the intravenous pump that will dispense the morphine which will separate Tim's mind from the pain in his body. Is there something to keep a mother sane while watching her child die?

Tim, as I stand and look at your peaceful face, the whole situation does not seem real to me. You are my youngest child. Can this really be happening? Are you going to leave this world before me? It doesn't seem right. It isn't natural.

It isn't right that we are alone this night. Your beloved Tom should be here. Tom, your partner, friend, companion and lover for six years, must be told. (Tom was serving as best man at his brother's wedding.) How ironic that he has been with you day and night through all of this terrible illness and on this night when he is gone, you are to be taken from him. I have to call him.

My mind is a muddle. Where did we leave the telephone number where Tom can be reached? Now I remember: it is on the dining room table at your home.

I can't leave you to go home and call Tom, but I know your best friend, Jeff, will take care of it. This poses another problem since I don't have his number either. I look at you. Are you really in a deep sleep? Will you hear me? Will you be able to respond?

I leaned over the bed and whispered, "Do you remember Jeff's telephone number?" Tim's mind never failed him and from his twilight sleep he recited Jeff's number.

Thankfully Jeff was home. After I explained the situation, he promised to come as quickly as possible to pick up the house key so he could get in and call Tom.

I am relieved. I pull the chair close to the bed and sit down. I reach over and clasp your hand. The strong pulse, the warmth of your skin and your rhythmic breathing belie the fact that you will be leaving soon.

The events of these last few hours are reborn in my mind. It had been a beautiful October Saturday. It is now evening. People are going about their business, performing their familiar late day rituals. The flowers are still blooming and the breezes are still gently blowing, but inside we are removed from everything except the tenuous life within these four walls on third floor west at Sherman Oaks Hospital.

## Reflections on the Day

I had made a quick trip to the grocery store that morning. I had been very mindful of the time because there was no attendant to be with Tim on Saturday. When I returned he seemed to be all right but didn't feel like eating lunch. The dilaudid shots seemed to be working, calming the pain as they were supposed to do and usually did.

As the afternoon wore on, he became more and more uncomfortable. Trips to the bathroom, although unproductive, were increasing in number. Now the dilaudid no longer worked, and he was crying out in pain and perspiring heavily. Those pain-numbing injections were needed at closer intervals, and he could no longer wait the prescribed three hours. I tried to reach Doctor Knight and got his service with a promise that he would call soon. I could do nothing to relieve Tim's suffering. After what seemed an eternity, but was actually a very short time, Dr. Knight called. After I explained the situation, he told me to give Tim another shot, even though it had been less than an hour since the last one, and if it didn't take effect to call him back. With hands a bit shaky, I administered the drug and prayed. There was a short respite from the pain, but only fifteen minutes later Tim was begging me for more, so I called Dr. Knight and his service promised he would call shortly. The pain intensified, and all I could do was hold Tim close to me and cry with him.

When Dr. Knight called back, he told us to go to the emergency room at the hospital and he would meet us there. By that time I am not sure Tim was fully aware of what was going on. As he got dressed the pain became unbearable. He screamed and pleaded for me to do some-thing—to give him another shot which would mean a few minutes' remission from the pain. My precious son, I couldn't allow anyone to suffer such agony, and although I realized that it could possibly kill him, I acquiesced and gave him a large dose.

Thankfully I managed to get him into the car. He was very quiet and out of it as we traveled along the Holly-wood Freeway to Sherman Oaks Hospital. Because traffic was light we got there in record time, in fact before Dr. Knight.

How Tim managed to get into the emergency room under his own power I still don't know, but he did. We were told there was no bed available and the doctor hadn't arrived yet, so we had to go into the waiting room where we were forced to be with other people during this diffi-cult time. There was a family waiting for their son's broken leg to be set. We waited while Tim was going into shock and his life was ebbing away. He no longer had pain, but he was very cold and his skin was developing a gray pallor.

I wondered if Tim would die, sitting on a chair in this room with his head on my shoulder. Each minute seemed like an hour—finally Dr. Knight walked in. He was angry and upset to find Tim sitting in the waiting area and helped him into an examining room where he gently probed and poked. Tim was still able to ask and answer questions, and Dr. Knight explained that his bowel had probably perforated and that this most certainly was the end of his life. He explained to Tim that he would be put on antibiotics (to prevent extensive infection) and morphine so he would have no more pain. Tim could request the amount of morphine needed to alleviate any discomfort. As Tim was taken to the elevator in a wheel chair, Dr. Knight looked at me with tears in his eyes and said, "I would like you to stay; he probably won't make it through the night." How much I appreciated this kind and compassionate human being who was a true friend as well as a fine doctor.

My mind is forced back to the present as Jeff comes to pick up the house key as promised. I am so appreciative of Tim's friends and their constant care. Jeff is one of the best. He shows his love and concern as he stands here with his arm around me and through his grief speaks softly to Tim. He reassures me that he will get in touch with Tom and that he will be there for all three of us when needed. His emotion is apparent as he leaves the room. This will be number three of those close to him that this disease has taken.

We are alone again. A nurse comes to check on you. Oh yes, the machines are working well, there is no pain, only the blessed numbness induced by the drug.

I look at you as you sleep peacefully under the influence of the morphine and I think, "Your face, once so fine and handsome, has been ravaged by the many months of illness. Thankfully the ugly purple lesions have not invaded your face. You are so very thin and your skin is stretched tightly over your aquiline nose, and the high cheekbones are emphasized because of the hollows below them. Your whole being creates a gaunt image that makes death seem imminent. Will you leave me tonight?"

In a short time Jeff calls and tells me he has reached Tom and that Tom would be here as soon as possible. "Oh, Tim, please don't leave until he gets here."

The hospital rooms are furnished with chairs which pull out to make beds. I am being removed from the reality of your struggle by the need to sleep. Mechanically I pull out the bed, crawl in between the sheets and sleep, absolutely exhausted by the day's events and the previous months of care.

# THREE

## Circumstances Of Love

### Other Hospitals

Tim and I had spent a great deal of time together in the hospital. He was born November 11, 1959, in a small town hospital in Minnesota. A big beautiful baby boy, seemingly perfect in every way. However, his eyes did not focus correctly at the proper age and were always drifting to the inner edge. After examination by a specialist we were told that his eye muscles were not simply weak but deformed and that surgery was the only way to correct the crossed eyes. Surgery would have to be performed very soon because it was apparent that one eye was being used more than the other and the sight could be lost in the lazy eye.

### Danville, Illinois, 1961

The first surgery would take place when Tim was fifteen months old. The eye specialist did his surgery at St. Elizabeth's Hospital. Tim looked so tiny as they wheeled him into surgery. While he was in surgery, all Dave and I could do was wait and pray. The procedure was not to be difficult or dangerous, but Tim was such a little boy. I couldn't help but think about all the what if's—he was so loving and trusting; would that trust still be there or would he learn at his tender age that there are so many ways to be hurt? He was finding out that even father and mother could not protect him from pain and even delivered him to his tormentors.

The Catholic sisters were very compassionate as they tried to comfort me. Knowing they were short-staffed, they encouraged me to spend the night. This was unusual in that I didn't find this kind of caring in the hospital when he had his last four eye surgeries.

When Tim awoke, both his eyes were bandaged and he was terrified. I held him close and he seemed to be reassured that although hurting he was safe.

I spent the night on a cot next to the crib in which my little boy slept. The night was long and dark as I lay listening to Tim's soft easy breathing. From the hall, the soft light and the hospital night sounds invaded the quiet of the room. Finally I slept.

## Sherman Oaks Hospital, Los Angeles, 1986

I wake to the sounds of the hospital and remember where I am and why. "Oh Tim, how much I would like to gather you in my arms and make things better, but I can't. Oh God, I have called you to heal (You said, no), to keep Tim from pain (You said, no), for the understanding of others (You said, some), for the strength to let go (You said, when it is time)." Through this I have come to understand that you rarely intervene in the human condition, but surely you grieve with us in our pain.

At last Jeff and Tom arrive. It has been an ordeal for Tom to get here. After the wedding reception there had been an impromptu party for friends and family to attend. Tom went to the party; however, the day's events had been enough for Tom's parents and they went back to the hotel for a good night's rest. It was Phil and Connie who found the message to call Jeff, so they got in touch with Tom immediately.

It was in this fashion, in the midst of the celebration of the uniting of two young lives that Tom heard that he might never see his beloved Tim again.

The stress of changing all plans, hassling airline flights, and his genuine grief was apparent when Tom walked into the room. He went to Tim immediately, and Tim realized that Tom was there. "Thank you, God."

**First Birthday (Before 1st Surgery)**

**Grandpa Loves Me**

**Music Soothes the Soul**

# FOUR

# For Being What You Are

## Danville, Illinois

When one considers what, as a small child, Tim must have gone through knowing there was something inside him that was not "normal" as well as his eyes not being quite right, and considering himself ugly and unloveable, there is no wonder his self-esteem was nonexistent.

While we lived in Illinois, he underwent his second eye surgery. The surgeon was working on the muscles gradually so as not to overcorrect. Overcorrection would have caused the eyes to pull to the outside (fish eyes) which at that time was very difficult to correct. By now Tim was adjusting to the doctors' examinations and probings as a normal part of his life.

While still very small Tim was already learning to be a loner. Pam and Mike were attending school, and, since there were no other children Tim's age in the neighborhood, he entertained himself. He had a small-pedal car, a jeep, which he would drive around the cul-de-sac on which we lived. One evening at dusk this little lone soldier in his jeep wandered a little too far down the block. A neighbor was backing out of his driveway and struck Tim's little jeep. I had asked Pam to keep her eye on him, so when I heard the crash I ran out and started screaming at Pam, "Why weren't you watching him? How could you let this happen?" I was unloading my own feelings of guilt on my daughter, which I know really hurt her in ways that would not be apparent for a long time. Forgive me, Pam.

Tim thankfully was not hurt; in fact, he wasn't even afraid, so the hospital was avoided that time.

Tim was fascinated with animals and since our old dachshund, Long Sam, had been so gentle (Long Sam died some time before), he believed in his childish innocence that all animals would tolerate what he considered loving play. The family next door had a big, old, yellow tomcat who made himself at home in any house he could get into. One morning a blood-curdling scream echoed throughout the house. I ran into the living room, and there sat Tim with blood running into his eyes from his forehead. He also had gashes on both sides of his head. The cat had not appreciated Tim's attentions and had grabbed him with his claws on both sides of his head and chewed his forehead.

This time a trip to the hospital was necessary, so I dispensed with the cat, grabbed Tim and a towel to hold over the wound on his forehead, and got to the hospital in record time. Sometimes I wonder if even this incident planted some seeds of rejection within Tim.

Everyone has to belong somewhere at some time, but

Tim found little acceptance in his early life.

Tim was my third child, and, in ways that I find difficult to express in words, he was simply different. Most of the differences were very subtle, but there seemed to be a premonition of trouble that made me anxious for him. As he got older it became more apparent that he had problems relating to other boys with their activities, and in the back of my mind I wondered if someday he would have problems with his sexuality. Then I would look at this precious little boy with all his childish innocence and think, "How silly. We are a good Christian family doing everything we can for God. The Lord wouldn't do this to us, would he? For what purpose? What did we have to learn?" With this in mind, I managed to gloss it over.

## Milwaukee, Wisconsin— One of the Gentle People

As a pre-schooler Tim was a gentle little boy who didn't like to roughhouse very much. His best friends were girls, so he learned to play with dolls and to relate to girls as buddies. He and his best friend, Karla, were inseparable, but Karla's mother died from cancer and Karla moved away. This was a major loss in his life.

He had other friends, some other little boys in the neighborhood, but we lived in an apartment complex where people were very transient, so if he made friends it wasn't long until the friend was gone.

The scouting programs were in danger of failing in this transient neighborhood because people didn't want the responsibility of a group of girls or boys in an apartment. I served as a leader for Pam's girl scout troop and as a den mother for Mike's pack of cub scouts. Tim was involved simply because he was there. The girls treated him like someone they would baby-sit with and the boys tolerated him, but he was still the fifth wheel, the one who didn't belong or was in the way—on the outside looking in.

Many things about Milwaukee were very good. We became part of a wonderful Baptist church that was just a fledging congregation. Almost all of the families were about the same age, were somewhat on a par financially, and were very compatible. Dave and I felt at home and secure in our relationships, becoming very active in every aspect of church life.

The children grew in their love for God and knowledge of the scriptures; they also seemed to have a great deal of fun. It was only in social situations such as picnics or parties that I could see Tim struggle. Even as he tried to compete in games with children of his own age, because of his lack of depth perception and co-ordination, he already was developing an "I can't" philosophy and the sense of being a loser.

There are beautiful memories of my children performing in the church, sometimes shy, sometimes radiant and at times too loud and enthusiastic as they sang about God's great love for all. There was such a sweetness and joy as they sang, **"Oh, How I Love Jesus"** and **"Jesus Loves Me."** Pam, Mike and Tim all believed it, and it is the truth for all of them, not one more than the other.

The last four eye surgeries took place in Milwaukee. The surgeon was a caring capable man who truly tried everything to fix Tim's eyes, but it would never be quite enough.

St. Michael's Hospital had a beautiful pediatrics wing (a contrast to St. Elizabeth's in Danville) but some very cruel and archaic rules. The hospital was understaffed as was St. Elizabeth's, but the rules would not allow parents to spend the night. So after the surgery Dave and I would be there when Tim came out of the anesthetic; however, in the dark of the night he would have to fight his nightmares alone.

In this macho world, being one of the gentle ones is not acceptable, and because of his eye problems he couldn't do "boy things." When little boys can't do something like hit, catch or bounce a ball, they are not very popular. Tim would just give up and walk away from the others wondering why he had to be different.

As the children got older, they didn't look kindly upon that gentle little boy with the horn rimmed glasses who couldn't keep up with them. From the first grade on, the boys thought it was great fun to label this odd little child with names like cross- eyes, girl, sissy, etc. Tim would cry and wonder why no one wanted to be his friend. He was beginning to believe the lie, the lie that he was not worthy to be loved and accepted.

It was during his early elementary years that I even entertained thoughts of having another child so Tim would have someone of his own to love and to love him. Then I would think that perhaps he would be rejected even by a younger sibling, and knowing that would only add to the pain, I decided against it.

**Touchdown**

**Lake Michigan:
"The Water's Cold"**

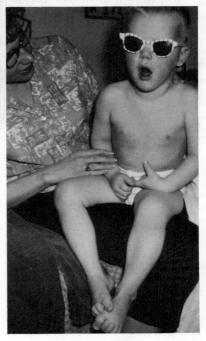

**Measles**

# FIVE

# A Different Drummer

## Minneapolis, Minnesota

Dave acquired a position with a printing firm in Minneapolis, Minnesota. I had sold Avon for many years and now was promoted to district manager in an older section of the city. This was a demanding position which required the majority of my time.

We all said goodbye to our friends again and moved into a beautiful two-story colonial house in the suburb of Brooklyn Park. We became members of Redeemer Covenant Church, where the pastor and staff were very personable and extremely concerned with the youth of the community. Pam and Mike were teenagers and found an extremely active youth group that functioned the year round. Tim joined in the Trail Blazer program for the younger children with great enthusiasm and through the years received many awards. Although he participated with all of his heart and soul, he never seemed to be a real part of the fabric that made up Redeemer's youth program.

In school Tim met another young man who was also left out of the mainstream of life because he had a minor physical impairment. John lived only a few houses from us, and he and Tim became fast friends. The two of them really didn't fit anywhere, although they tried. At one point we parents almost forced them into a wrestling program which they faithfully attended each week. When the final tournaments came, Tim lost his event and because John's opponent didn't show up, he was awarded a medal. This served only to make Tim feel less viable as a real boy. No amount of praise for his attempt made any difference. He knew he had failed again.

Mike was so interested in sports that he had more in common with his father than Tim did. Dave served as coach for Little League softball and football teams in which he coached Mike. He thought that by being coach he could make Tim comfortable with sports, so he enlisted Tim for the football team.

Dave made a valiant effort, but Tim was so convinced that he was a loser at anything physical that he proved himself right, a self-fulfilling prophecy.

When softball season came around, Tim did not want anything to do with it, but Dave insisted he try. This is where I tried to intervene, telling Dave that with Tim's perceptual problems he could not possibly hit or catch a ball. On one level I think Dave understood this, and yet at another level I think he wanted so much for Tim to succeed in some sport that he forced the issue, saying that I was babying Tim and trying to protect him.

I readily admit to trying to protect Tim from any more failures. I cried and pleaded, but Dave wouldn't listen, so he dragged Tim off to another humiliating experience where his limitations were put on display for all to see.

Not fitting in or being one of the boys had a positive side, however, as Tim spent a great deal of time reading and concentrating on his music. He also experimented with chemistry sets and created wonderful inventions with electronic equipment. He and John used their imaginations with space toys and plastic army men to put together a fantasy world that they could control.

At this point another young man moved into the neighborhood. Roman was younger and had some emotional problems which kept him outside of the established social structures, so he fit with John and Tim very well.

I was finding it increasingly difficult to balance a demanding job and a family. One evening as I was talking to one of my sales representatives on the phone, Tim was writing with his magic markers. He left the table and when the conversation was over, I hung up and looked to see what Tim had been writing. On the paper was written in large red letters, "I HATE AVON."

This confirmed the negative feelings I had been having about being both a career women and a mother. My family was not being taken care of. I had given Pam at age 13 an adult responsibility, my responsibility. She was expected to keep track of Mike and Tim all the time I was out of the house, and the boys, particularly Mike, would not cooperate. One day she came to me saying, "Mom, I don't care if we are poor, but you have to stay home."

All of my children were giving me the message that they needed me at home; they needed a full-time mother. Although it was difficult to give up my job, it was also a big relief. My baggage of guilt and stress was lightened considerably.

## Puppy Love

We had a large house with ample yard and now that I would be at home, I thought about getting a dog. Dogs had been some of my best friends when I was a child, so I believed that to have a loving, loyal, cute and cuddly puppy might prove beneficial for all of the children, particularly Tim.

Some of the family had allergies, so we had to be careful which breed of dog we brought into our home. Cock-a-poos were a fad at the time and since they were cute and didn't shed very much, they seemed to be a perfect choice. After calling many pet stores I finally found one that had some little cock-a-poos, or so they said. I didn't have any reason to doubt them when I saw these loveable puppies. They were brown but had some gray kinky hair standing out, which in my mind said cocker and poodle.

My oldest son, Mike, went with me to pick out the puppy with which to surprise Tim. He chose a curious little female that would make us forget that she was a mongrel. (As the dog grew, the vet and I realized that there was neither cocker or poodle in the dog—she was a beagle mix.)

Tim came home from school that day and the puppy climbed all over him. It was love at first sight for both of them. Tim and Mike wanted to name her, but the name had to be something special for this very special little dog. They had a hard time deciding between Cinnamon and Ginger but decided Ginger was easier to say when calling her. So Ginger it was.

Ginger didn't care if Tim's eyes weren't perfect or that he wasn't coordinated. It was Tim's gentleness, care and love for the little animal that truly made Ginger Tim's dog. This is the way it was until many years later when we moved to Lindsborg, Kansas and Tim moved to New York City; at that time she became my dog.

## A Part of the Congregation

With more time at my disposal I could get more involved with church work. Jan, the pastor's wife, and I decided that we could have a teen choir in our church, so along with Mary, a wonderful friend and pianist, we announced the first practice. Thirty young people showed up, eager to participate. Jan was the director, Mary the accompanist, and Dave and I were organizers and order-keepers. No one had to try out, just be committed to making the choir the best it could be.

Pam and Mike were part of the group (Mike playing first his guitar and later the string bass), but Tim wasn't quite old enough. He was in fifth grade and even though he had been chosen for the select choir at school, he would have to wait for junior high to be in the church group.

The choir grew and I was looking forward to the time when Tim could be part of this wonderful, exciting musical group. Finally the time came. He was eager as he practiced with the group and looked forward to the performances and to the trips we made each year. However, that little difference that shone forth from Tim kept him from the true fun and fellowship that most young people experienced with the teen choir.

While traveling, partners would have to be chosen when spending the night at private homes, and we adults would have to put Tim in with someone because he wouldn't be chosen and he didn't have a special buddy in the group. Again, Tim was never truly accepted, nor was he part of the inner circle where his brother and sister were.

One time the group was traveling and had a few free hours. I wondered what Tim would do if he was left alone. I thanked God when I saw the pastor's son Jeff and his friends ask Tim to come with them. My heart fell when I learned that the Pastor had forced them to include Tim. He tagged along with them without feeling that they really wanted him.

One beautiful summer day Pastor Al and Jan invited the Youth Groups and some parents to their lake cottage for a day of food, fun and fellowship. The older children were water skiing while some of the junior high kids, equipped with life jackets, took the rowboats out. Tim was not included, so he had to pretend he didn't care and tried to show enthusiasm as he asked me to go out in the boat with him.

Pam and Mike were both involved in a very fine and stringent confirmation program and were confirmed by Pastor Al. However, before Tim had that opportunity we knew we would be moving again, this time to Denver.

Minneapolis had been a nice place to live. We had many good friends and wonderful fellowship in the church. We had the love and support of our families who lived close by. Our children had experienced having hands-on grandmas and grandpas as well as aunts, uncles and cousins. This would be sorely missed. Since Pam was away at college, our move would mean that she would no longer have a familiar home to come back to. Mike, who was a senior in high school with many friends and very active in sports and music, truly did not want to leave.

Then there was Tim, who always excelled in academics and music, who had a paper route he had so faithfully built and his small circle of friends, who now would again have to try to find a place for himself. Of course there was always a chance that things would be better, that he truly might be a part of something, really belong somewhere.

**Florida Trips**

# SIX

# A Part Of The Journey

## Denver, Colorado

At the time we moved to Littleton, a suburb of Denver, a family from Oklahoma moved in across from us. Tim and their son, Ross, became good friends and shared many common interests. Ross was a fine young man who learned to know Tim and accepted him for who he was, and what anyone else thought didn't seem to matter. Ross had a terrific self-image and was an extremely confident person who knew he belonged wherever he wanted to be.

One Fourth of July, Tim and Ross were using some firecrackers while playing army, and since fireworks were illegal in that particular suburb, a neighbor called the police. The police hauled these two young men off to the station and we, the parents, were called to come and get them. We never saw two more terrified young men in our lives. If all young people could have an experience like this it would probably deter them from any future criminal activity.

When school started and Tim began the eighth grade we realized that circumstances were not going to be any better for Tim in this school system. Ross was a year younger, so he had no classes with Tim.

Man's inhumanity to man became more apparent when these "children" reached junior high age. It seemed that so many would do anything to make themselves look important and to find their place in the pecking order. In Tim they found someone who couldn't or wouldn't fight back and ganged up on him, making jokes at his expense, calling him names—oh yes, … the names now became more cruel and explicit, such as fairy, fag, queer and homo. It was going to be another lonely time for Tim because even if he was an all right guy, the voice of peer pressure spoke with authority as to who associates with whom.

Winter in Colorado could be very rough, but Tim would ride his bike to school in good and bad weather rather than suffer the pain inflicted upon him during the bus ride. Gym class was torture, for as he had little coordination and no depth perception his inadequacies were painfully apparent. Tim was always the last one to be chosen.

His imagination now knew no bounds and he became increasingly creative. He read, he wrote, he continued being fascinated by electronics and made up elaborate space fantasies. Doug, my future son-in-law, was in the building trade, and he helped Tim build a space ship in our back yard. It was a large structure with room enough for three to four young people. It had a realistic control panel inside and was painted a gleaming metallic silver.

For a time our yard was the busiest in the neighborhood, and Tim thought at last he had some friends, but as the interest faded so did those friendships. Tim spent many nights out in that ship, wrapped in a sleeping bag, creating a world of his own where he was someone important and where he truly had a place.

During that period of time he read a great deal and wrote science fiction, creating his own better world. He immersed himself in music, but even though he was recognized for his talent, he would look in the mirror and see the cross-eyed effeminate sissy who just didn't belong. He never realized what a handsome, talented and gifted person he was; he could only see the flaws.

Tim and Ross belonged to a Boy Scout troop which proved to be one of the more positive happenings in Tim's life. It was a place where he became more outgoing and self confident. The troop was made up of boys who didn't have to put anyone down to feel secure about themselves. Tim seemed to gain self-confidence as he participated and found that he could do things that up to this time he wouldn't even try.

I remember one June day when the boys were to go camping in the mountains. It was raining in Littleton as Dave and I and the other drivers started for the campsite with a load of teen-age boys. By the time we started up into the mountains it was lightly snowing, and when we reached the campsite it was a full-blown blizzard. We let the boys off and wished them and their scout leaders best of luck. The pass we had crossed on our way up was now closed, so we had to take another way home. The boys spent a long weekend in the snow storm and survived very well and seemingly enjoyed every minute of it.

Another ego-building experience for Tim occurred when the youth leader from our church took a few junior high boys on a winter excursion in the mountains that today would rival an outward- bound experience. They roughed it by carrying their gear during the day and sleeping in tents at night. They didn't take very many supplies because they were going to camp near a lake and fish for food. A storm made the lake inaccessible and their climbing precarious at best. When they arrived home, exhausted and hungry, Rick said they had all proved themselves as men. If it hadn't been for their cooperation and urging each other on, they probably wouldn't have made it. Tim had crossed another hurdle.

**He's not heavy, he's our brother**

# SEVEN

# Love In All Circumstances

## Insensitive Mother and Father

During Tim's sophomore year we made a family trip to California and stayed at a motel in Laguna Beach which, unknown to us at that time, is a gay man's paradise. We made excursions to Disneyland, Knotts Berry Farm and Universal City, and although it was rather cold and damp, we enjoyed the beach together as a family.

One evening Tim failed to come in at curfew time. We were almost hysterical and ready to call the police when Tim walked in looking fine. I really don't know what happened that night, but I think Tim found out he wasn't alone in his feelings and he found acceptance somewhere on the beach.

# A SONG

(A poem by Tim,
written sometime in his sophomore year)

*Sand flying high, kicked up by bare feet;*
*Water splashing from tide,*
*Sun radiating gentle heat.*

*Laughing, running, a teasing shove into the*
*waves,*
*Hand in Hand, playing wrestling inside caves.*

*A kiss, a touch, intimate affection from*
*devotion,*
*An embrace, never letting go,*
*Grasping at a lasting emotion.*

*Love on the Beach,*

*It seemed too far to reach,*
*And yet I've learned to teach*
*Sweet music by the sea.*

*Sunset drew near, colors flew by our side;*
*Together, forever and ever,*
*Had it not been for high tide.*

*Walking, swimming, a few precious moments*
*of play,*
*Arm in Arm, walking, leaving only footprints*
*by the bay.*

*A moon, a glance, sea gulls crying off the shore,*
*A tear, goodbye, night beckons no more.*

*Love on the Beach*

*It seemed too far to reach,*
*And yet I've learned to teach,*
*Sweet music by the sea.*

*Love on the Beach*

*It was too far to reach,*
*And now I've learned to teach,*
*That there's nothing but the sea.*

Because we didn't understand and didn't know better, as we drove out of Laguna Beach, Dave and I raved on about the morals of the homosexuals as we saw them playing volleyball and just enjoying each other's company. We said it was a cop-out by men who just didn't want to face responsibility for a family as God meant it to be. (Knowing deep in my heart that Tim was troubled by his differences, I thought if a choice was to be made, if enough negative pressure was applied, Tim would be able to choose the right path. How little I knew about choice in this matter.) We really let out all of our prejudices over and over in front of Tim. I know now how terrible he must have felt, afraid to acknowledge what he was because then he might not even be acceptable to Mom and Dad. Then no one would love him.

## High School, A Good Beginning

High school looked promising. Tim became involved in theatre and was chosen to be a Madrigal singer, which was quite an honor in a school of 2,500.

He started to date girls and I was so relieved. "Thank You, God, I knew I could trust you." However, this wasn't to be; it was just a cover, a try at being "normal," not the real thing.

During the Christmas season all of the Madrigal singers would come to our house for cocoa and food after caroling around the neighborhood. Tim really seemed to fit in and have fun, which made me extremely happy. Tim was in every respect a part of this group of young people.

## Out Of The Closet

As a sophomore Tim became involved with Bob, a senior boy who upon graduation dumped Tim and let everyone in school know what Tim was. He had nothing to lose because he was leaving town and going to college out of state. It was after this episode that Tim attempted suicide. Two young men in the Madrigals and theatre group brought Tim home.

Tim was inconsolable. He wanted to move away—anywhere. Then he said to Dave and me, "Mom and Dad, I am a hopeless homosexual." He didn't know how we would react or if he would even have a home after he "came out."

## ANGRY SEA

*The wind snaps and whirls about,*
*across the angry sea*
*In the air, dark cumulus clouds whirl*
*about to create*
*An everlasting oblivion.*

*Time passes ... years are seconds,*
*centuries minutes ... but the clouds and*
*the angry sea play a ritualistic game with*
*each other, always twirling, dancing, but*
*never changing ... the same ... the same,*

*No other sound except the wind and waves ...*
*the same ... the same ... through*
   *eternity ...*

   *Float on by ... Float on by ...*

*Take me to the oblivion where it is alive,*
*yet there is no life, Where there is playful*
*anger which never ceases.*

Tim Barbo

It was at the moment of Tim's disclosure that a miracle occurred. Dave had always had a terrible temper which could be very destructive and hurtful. If he had reacted in his normal way, he would have struck Tim and thrown him out. However, the reaction of the natural man did not come to pass. It was as if God said to him, "You would accept your child under any other circumstances, why not this one? If he were crippled in any other way, you would still love him, why not now?"

How could his father and I being "good Christians" accept this lifestyle for one of our own? We fought it as much as possible by going to our pastor for help and then to Christian Counseling, but this was a futile struggle for we are frail human beings and each of us has our own struggle in this life, Tim's being one of the greatest.

Tim asked Dave and me if we could change our sexual

preference. We realized that would be impossible, so we began to understand and accept things as they were.

As Tim experienced one painful rejection after another, I came very close to hating Bob. It had to be the Spirit of God that gave me release from the hate, and a concern for what that young man was going to experience in life. After all, when Tim had no one else, he had God. We had no idea if Bob had any beliefs at all, so for his graduation we gave him a collection of the writings of C. S. Lewis.

However, as a mother, my sadness for my son was overwhelming. Any time of the day, doing the most mundane things, my emotions would spill over in the form of tears. Sometimes it would be on the street, or in the supermarket as I observed young couples in love, or watched young families with their children. I would think, "Tim will never know that kind of love—he will never have a family of his own." Then I would have to turn my face until I could gain control once more.

At this time I could not confide in my mother and father or brother or sister. Yes, I felt sad for Tim, but I also felt ashamed. How could something like this happen in our family? What had we done wrong? These were normal feelings for us as parents until we accepted God's invitation to grow and learn unconditional love.

I had a good true friend to whom I could tell anything and she would listen to me and never judge me or my son. She was truly my source of sanity in this nightmare time of my life. "Thank you, Penny."

Tim built a wall around himself and by keeping himself hardened to cruel comments and at arms length from other people he finished his sophomore year. One by one his friends turned from him. Often he would say, "I wish I could be with someone; I wish I had a true friend." Finally it was, "I don't need anyone." The change had begun.

Summer was upon us and Tim found a job as bus boy at the Denver Country Club. He worked hard and did a good job, but he was extremely lonely. He worked late at night, and when he came home he wanted to talk, so I would stay up and be available to listen.

One night he came home very distraught. A sheet of paper had been put under the windshield wiper of his car with announcements of gay activities in the area. He didn't know how anyone had found out his secret as he was trying so desperately to keep it to himself.

The rest of Tim's high school years found him lonely most of the time. He was always in a defensive position, acting as though he didn't care what others thought and fitting in the best he could. His grades were good; he was involved in the music program of the school, and he even had dates for the Junior and Senior Proms. As I look back, I know some of his friends were good friends and would have been there for him if he had let them.

The church always played a large part in Tim's life. In the Baptist church we attended in Littleton, Tim took part in the music as a member of the "Son Seekers," and was Faithful in a dramatic rendition of Pilgrim's Progress. He regularly attended Sunday school and church until the black and white, narrow line of thinking conflicted with what and who Tim was and what he had perceived as the truth through what God allowed in his life.

The church had three pastors at that time, and Dave and I went to them for some help, encouragement, consolation and understanding. Dave went to the Youth Pastor and wept for our son. We found out then that pastors are ill prepared to deal with this situation. They dealt with it by disbelief and denial, such as: Christian families shouldn't have these problems, or ignore it and maybe it will go away. In defense of the Senior Pastor, before we moved from Littleton to Lindsborg, he called me in saying, "Would you come in and talk to me; I think I need some education." So I went in and talked about Tim, his life and what all of this meant to us as a Christian family. I think he really listened to me, heard, and tried to be open to a new understanding. There were others in the congregation who were having some of the same problems as Tim with the sexuality issue. I hope the pastors were more help to them than they were to us.

Our perception of God and truth was being changed, and our hearts and minds were being challenged by the meaning of love and acceptance through Christ as this situation was allowed in our lives. We no longer required that Tim attend "our church" every time the doors opened.

Helping Dad

Now I Lay Me
Down to Sleep

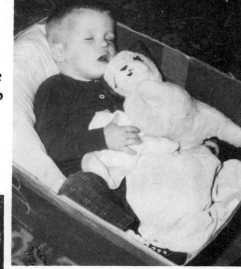

Merry Christmas

# Happy Birthday, Dear Timmy

# EIGHT

# "And Who Will Cast The First Stone?"

One Saturday Tim said to me, "Mom, I know you are concerned about my life style and where I spend my evenings on the weekends. Will you come to a Gay Bar with me?" This was going to be quite an experience for a middle-class, Christian housewife and mother whose values had always been very conservative. Now my view of life was being stretched and expanded by this special child God had trusted me with.

I went with Tim and his friend, Gary. We walked in the door and my apprehension fell away. It was like any other bar I imagined (not having frequented very many) except that everyone there was male with the exception of four women.

There was nothing unusual going on. The young men (and some not so young) were drinking (no one was drunk or obnoxious) and dancing, but most of all just talking in

55

a general atmosphere of congeniality.

I had a wonderful time. Almost everyone asked me to dance, and some were comfortable enough to share their life stories with me. I think I represented a mother figure for many and they trusted me to accept them.

There was a young man from Kansas who told me that he had just written to his parents to tell them that he was homosexual. He didn't know if he would ever be allowed in their home again. He said, "I prayed for years that God would change me. I knew that there was something wrong with me and that I wasn't an acceptable human being because of the feelings I had for men and boys that I should have had for women and girls. As I was active in a Baptist church, I begged and bargained with God to make me straight. It didn't happen. I have been engaged twice thinking that marriage might fix me; however, I knew that wasn't the answer and I would end up ruining the woman's life and my own. Finally I have to make peace with who and what I am and must get on with my life."

He told me that he had just returned from the gay pride parade in Wichita, Kansas. He said. "the press always zeros in on the extremists, the guys dressed in women's clothing and those that are very militant. How much I would have liked to have gone up to the television reporter and said: My name is Ken; I am a Christian; I am a teacher and I love my job. I participate in community activities and try to be of service to society, and by the way, I am a homosexual. However, I couldn't do that because I would probably be rejected by my parents (at the time they didn't know). My friends would probably desert me. I might be thrown out of my apartment and I most certainly would lose my job."

A young man from the Middle East told me, "If my father knew, he would kill me." This young man never would be able to confide in his family if he wanted to go on living.

Another young man said, "I have been disowned by my family, they don't want to see me again. I asked if I could come home for Christmas. They said, 'No.' My Christian family."

From another, "My father disinherited me, won't acknowledge me as his son. My mom will still talk to me, but they are sending money to Anita Bryant."

And still another who was being "kept" by someone else: "I had to leave home, my father couldn't handle it. I don't have my High School diploma but I hope to get my G.E.D. so I can get a better job and live on my own."

I met an older couple who had recently moved to Denver from Houston. One of them had been offered a tremendous opportunity and promotion with his company. His partner had left his place of employment to come with him. The gentleman, who was on his way up in the business world, was very nice, attractive, and in no way would anyone know he was a homosexual. The partner was also very nice and attractive; however, he had so many effeminate characteristics that I knew he would have an extreme problem getting employment because of the common prejudice against anyone who might possibly be gay.

The recurrent theme through many of these lives was

the rejection by family when they were honest about themselves. So many preferred to live the lie and not have to face that rejection. (Many families know, but if it isn't said, it isn't so.) My heart goes out to these young men whose only offense is that they are different in one area of life.

"How much farther is God going to lead me into experiencing the pain of this segment of society?" It is a good thing I didn't know the answer to that question at the time.

Tim grew strong and more sure of himself in his senior year of high school. I think one gets stronger or perishes under the pressure of hiding who you are. He became a more assertive and aggressive person, which had a positive effect on his life in general. No one was ever going to walk over this kid again.

While in school, Tim had signed up with a talent agency which also offered some training in the field of performance particularly aimed at bit parts or extras in movies and commercials. He did get a small but paying part in **"One On One"** with Robby Benson. We had to look closely to see him, but he was one of the basketball players seated at the table, eating a meal. (Now whenever we see that movie we will have a brief glimpse of Tim and have him back with us for a fleeting moment.)

To make some money he got a job with Sears, demonstrating a new line of cookware. His sales presentation could almost be called theatrical, and he sold lots of pots and pans. His new self-assuredness surfaced again in a telemarketing position. He called people for consumer surveys, and his record of responses was greater than most.

One day, six weeks before he was to graduate from high school, we clashed over our house rules. We couldn't reach any agreement, so Tim took some of his clothes and in the heat of anger he left home and went to live with a friend. When he first left home, Dave and I didn't know where he was and we were frantic. We were very fortunate in that his friend trusted and respected us, so he called and told us where Tim was and kept us posted as to what was going on. Tim's plan was to quit school, get a job, work full time and get his G.E.D. Knowing how this would affect him and his whole future, Dave and I backed down so Tim came back on his own terms and finished high school.

Mike was home from college for Tim's graduation. One morning we were sitting at the kitchen table talking, with the television on in the background. The Donahue Show came on, and that day it was featuring a homosexual couple who were talking about their long-term relationship and what it had been like for them as they were growing up.

I looked at Mike and said, "You realize that your brother has this problem, don't you?" He appeared to be surprised and answered simply, "No." That was all he said, and he left the kitchen. There was no response from Mike for about two weeks; then one night he came and spoke to Dave and me as he sat at the foot of our bed. He said, "Mom and Dad, I have been thinking about Tim's situation and I have only two choices. I can reject Tim as my brother and as a human being, or I can hang in there with Tim, you and God, and that is what I have decided to do." Now that the truth was out, Mike showed more care and compassion for his brother than when he thought Tim was just moody and defensive.

Tim was never able to compete with Mike in any sport because of his eye problem; however, Tim had become an excellent skier. One day Mike and Tim were going skiing together for the first time. They went to Winter Park and were going to ski a very difficult run called Mary Jane. As they were coming down the mountain a ski patrol called Mike off the mountain because his skills were not quite up to the level of difficulty that run presented. Dave and I had always been thrilled with Mike's physical ability, but now we were extremely happy for Tim as he finally was better than Mike at something athletic.

Shortly after Tim's "coming out," Pam was bringing me home after an evening of shopping. (She and Doug were married by that time.) I knew I had to tell her, but how does a mother explain to a tender-hearted daughter that her little brother is gay? How could she understand what it all meant when I didn't understand?

Tears flooded our eyes as we held each other and wept for Timothy. Pam's love bridged the chasm between the perception of how things should be and the reality of our circumstances.

# NINE

## Finding His Way

### Los Angeles to New York

The Hollywood of the movies, promising fame and fortune, beckoned, so, after finishing high school, Tim drove our Vega to Los Angeles. He stayed at the YMCA while hunting for a job.

Life in L.A. is a hassle, as I found out in my later visits. Tim parked his car in a restricted zone one day, and it was towed away. The fine was so large he couldn't afford to retrieve the car, and everyday the fine got larger. He finally found a job and then called us and asked to borrow enough money to get the car. Now that he was employed he could pay us back.

One day during his job search he got on a bus in his gray three-piece suit. Somehow he missed his stop and ended up in Watts. Being very blond and dressed to the nines, he was feeling a little uncomfortable on the bus with all the blacks dressed in everyday casual garb. When he told that story, he said that although he was a minority as a homosexual, now he knew what it was like to be a conspicuous minority.

Eventually he became disillusioned with the Hollywood hype and its false promises, so he came home and worked for awhile with his dad at Youth For Christ.

Tim was looking for a career that would not be biased against homosexuals. He was a very creative and talented young man, so he decided to go to beauty school. From the beginning he was very good at hair design and also with the customers, so we cheered him on. We were happy because he seemed to be happy.

Dave lost his job, and the printing business in Lindsborg, Kansas (where our son Mike had attended college), became available on the market, so we sold our house, bought the business and moved. Tim knew he wouldn't be happy in a small town, so he moved to New York City to finish beauty school.

## New York to Kansas

The gay community is tantamount to a large family. Tim knew two people in New York, and they put him up until he found his own place. Being in school left very little money for living expenses, but he found a room in the Greek section of New York. When he wrote he told us how much he enjoyed the Greek customs and festivities that were a part of the ethnic culture of that area. (He also found out just how large cockroaches can grow.)

Even though he had friends around, Tim was leading an isolated existence. There was no one he was really close to because he didn't have a special person in his life, and his family was very far away. Although we had our differences, there was a deep love and affection between us and we missed each other greatly. However, I would be less than honest if I said that there weren't positive aspects about Tim being removed from our everyday lives. "Absence may make the heart grow fonder," but it also kept from us the immediate problems Tim was experiencing. To some extent another old maxim is true, "What we didn't know, didn't hurt us" ... as much.

Loneliness brought Tim into a closer walk with his God. He consistently studied and searched the scriptures for God's leading in his life. His letters told us that, as he studied, he considered the lives of the early Christians and how their trials made his look small. Dave and I were so thankful that Tim had not turned his back on God and all of his early upbringing.

He finished school and called us asking if he could come home. Selfishly my thoughts were, "Oh God, not again. I don't know if I can take anymore. I can't live being so intimately involved in his life that I am hurt every time he is hurt. I can't take any more rejection of my son. How much more can he take? I am tired and at the end of me. Help me! Help him!"

With a great deal of apprehension we told him, "Of course you can come home." Dave drove to New York, packed the car with all of Tim's belongings and brought him home to Lindsborg. It was good to see him again. He never went back to take his state boards because he knew he didn't want to make hair styling his life's work.

While he was in New York a friend gave him the book,

**"Your Erroneous Zones"** by Duane Dyer. This was one of the greatest gifts he ever received because it convinced him that he could take charge of his life and that he didn't have to allow other people to be a negative influence on him. Then Tim turned around and gave me that gift by telling me that I didn't have to worry about his happiness anymore. He said that he had taken control of his life, and whether or not he was happy was his responsibility. It was as though a weight had been lifted from my shoulders as I saw my son become a responsible man in charge of his own destiny.

Tim got a job in accounting at Sears in Salina, Kansas, where he learned to use a computer. This skill, along with his fine work record, was to be a great asset in his future employment searches. At this point of his life Tim got along very well with people and he had many friends, both straight and gay.

Our house became a place where his friends felt free to visit. One young man, along with his dog, lived with us while he got settled in a job and found a place to live. As I look back, I treasure the relationships that Dave and I built with the people in the gay community. It has been an enriching experience.

In the fall Tim started school at Bethany College. He did fine academically, but small-town life wasn't for him, so at semester break he transferred to Kansas University at Lawrence where he found a place for himself in a large and varied student body.

Tim's Growing-up Years —
One of the gentle people!

**Laguna Beach:**

**Tom introduced
Tim to a
love of Flowers!**

# TEN

# To Be Loved – To Belong

## San Francisco

Still the big city was where he wanted to be, so after finishing the second semester he went to San Francisco and got a job with Pacific Bell Telephone. He had come into his own—he was his own person.

Being thrust into a community where you are accepted for who you are and what you can do, with none of the negative connotations of your sexual preference, must be a culture shock for someone like Tim, who up to this point knew who and what he was but didn't know what to do about it. I believe that it is in this situation of finally being accepted and being among those like you, that sexual excesses do occur. There seemed to be no consequences, therefore no limits on sexual activity. For those who feel like a blemish on society, a little more bruising doesn't matter. At last he belonged somewhere.

It is possible that it was in this setting that the modern-day plague began in this country. It was probably at that time that Tim contracted the disease that would stay hidden for so many years and that eventually took his life.

There was a great deal of pressure in his job, but he took it in stride and was very good at it. This was a great source of satisfaction to him. He lived in a beautiful section of San Francisco where the gay community was buying and refurbishing old row houses. It was becoming a showplace and an example of what beauty can be restored to an old area.

Tim was renting a large bedroom on the second floor of an old row house on Delores Street. One whole side of the room was given over to a huge bay window which allowed the room to be flooded with sunshine. Tim had kitchen privileges, so he did all of his own cooking. The kitchen was a large old-fashioned room with a porch that overlooked the city. The view at night was spectacular.

Dave and I paid a visit to our son in his new home and had a wonderful time. We toured the neighborhood and marveled at the wonderful old houses. We visited the Wharf and the famous Pier 57. Tim took us to some parks and over the Golden Gate bridge to the area north of San Francisco where we enjoyed the beach, ocean and sun.

When we returned home from the beach, Tim had clothes to wash, so he asked me to go with him to a laundromat on Castro Street. As we walked down the street there were many couples, mostly male, and although the street was crowded I was one of very few women. Everyone was so kind and courteous to me that I felt very special.

## Tom – Another Son

It was on this visit that we were introduced to Tim's special friend, Tom. Both of these young men were tired of life in the fast lane and the meaningless relationships. They were both separately praying for that special person, a Christian, whom they could make a total commitment to. I believe that God intended that they meet. Dave and I fell in love with Tom immediately, and as they started their life together we looked on it as a marriage. We had another son.

Tim was promoted and would have to move to Los Angeles, so Tom sought transfer to the Los Angeles branch of the well-known brokerage house for which he worked. They found a garage that had been converted into a bungalow in Laguna Beach. It was small but delightful. Tom loved growing things, so there were flowers in colorful abundance. Cats also seemed to find a second home at this charming little house, so there were always one or two felines sunning themselves among the flowers.

**Wedding picture: Pam and Doug**

**Wedding picture: Mike and Sherri**

# $\mathcal{A}$ New Chapter – $\mathcal{A}$ New Life

## Tim and Tom

Things seemed to be going well as Tim's and Tom's personalities seemed to complement each other. Tim was the aggressive businessman who carefully watched their finances, and Tom was the gentle nurturer. As time went on they learned from each other as Tim became a more caring person and Tom became more assertive.

Tom had never officially "come out" to his parents, so he thought that it was something he had to do. He wanted Tim to come to his parents' home near Portland, Oregon, so that they could meet Tim. They called me and told me what they were going to do. I said, "Wait a minute and reconsider what you are doing and how you are doing it. Tom's folks have no idea what your lives are about. This is going to be a big shock, so don't be surprised by the reaction they might have. This is a lot to drop on them all at once. When you tell them, give them a chance to adjust, don't expect instant acceptance."

To make matters worse, Tim was going through one of his non-conformist periods at the time, so when he wasn't at work he dressed very casually (not Ivy League to say the least), and he also had a little tail of hair in the back that was so popular a few years ago. He was not the picture of the ideal young man a daughter should bring home, much less a son.

When they arrived Tim was introduced as a friend and they settled into Tom's old bedroom. The first few days nothing more was said, but one morning near the end of their visit, Tom's father left a note on the refrigerator door. It said, "Meet me for lunch – we have to talk." Phil didn't want to accept that his son was gay or the reality of Tim's and Tom's relationship. He finally conceded that if it was the only way Tom could be, and it made Tom happy, he could handle it. I call this another miracle.

Sometime later, there was an emergency trip to Minnesota when Tim was called upon to be a pallbearer at Dave's mother's funeral. Grandma Barbo had requested that all of her grandsons participate in this manner. He flew in from San Francisco the day before the services, and we all stayed at the home of Dave's sister in the small town where the service would take place.

Tim was at a point in his life where he was somewhat uncomfortable away from his peers. The association with his extended family at this time made him very uneasy because he had to play his little charade again.

It was a very emotional time as he viewed his grandmother in her casket. This was the first time as an adult that Tim faced the reality of death. Of course this was the death of an old woman; nevertheless, it was someone he cared about. It was a confrontation with mortality. But being the healthy young man that he was, it seemed as though he had limitless time.

Our son Mike was getting married December 27th, 1980. Dave and I loved his fiancee, Sherri, and were so happy to be getting another daughter. Tim was coming from Los Angeles to be best man for his brother. Dave was to meet him at the Kansas City airport the evening of the 26th for the drive to Hays, Kansas, and the wedding rehearsal. The plane was late, so they missed the rehearsal and even came late to the rehearsal dinner. This unknown delay and lateness of the hour had me concerned. When they walked in it was obvious that Tim was still making a statement about who he was. He had a very "Los Angeles butch" look, wearing black leather vest and pants, with black leather boots, and the tail of hair was still there.

To be honest I was somewhat embarrassed because I knew how great he looked dressed up in suit and tie. I knew how he dressed for work and felt that he could have shown enough respect to dress appropriately. Whatever his brother or anyone else thought, they kept it to themselves, so I became more comfortable with the situation too. This was my problem—worrying about what people would think. Yes, I was embarrassed for me and, on the other hand, I didn't want any more rejection for Tim, even though he was asking for it. It was as though he was defiantly saying, "Accept me for who I am, even though I do not fit your mold." He was very polite and gracious, delighted to meet Sherri, and friendly to everyone. So the trappings and outward appearances did not matter anymore, for it was not a reflection of the heart. Our family had a chance to renew our relationships, and the wedding took place without incident the next day.

When Tim and Tom met, Tom had an old convertible which they called "Miss Parklane." This was Tom's most precious possession. Often they would get into the car and drive around with the top down enjoying the beautiful California countryside, the all-encompassing warmth of the ever-present sun, but most of all, each other's company.

They each brought some belongings into the relationship, and with each move they had to add some new things. There were many promotions which entailed different offices, so they made the appropriate concessions. Sometimes Tom would move because of Tim's opportunity and when the situation was in Tom's favor, Tim would move.

Each place they moved to truly became a home. Whether it was an apartment or a house, they were very good at making it their place. When they were in need of some new furniture, they would go out and find it; then because Tim's eye was always on the budget, they would wait until it was on sale before they would buy it. This drove Tom crazy. Tom always added some special colorful touches with his flowers and plants.

They shared some very wonderful times together. On special occasions such as birthdays and anniversaries they would give each other red gladiolas and go out to a fine restaurant to eat. Each restaurant would become their special place because another year of their life and relationship was celebrated there.

His eye problem was to make a great impact and create obstacles in Tim's life that he never really overcame. After going through the trauma of six surgeries, his eyes were almost, but not quite normal. They would wander when he became tired.

It wasn't until about a year into their relationship that Tom found out about Tim's feelings of rejection because of his eyes. He had no idea there was even a problem. Every time they would go out together, no matter how much fun they were having, as soon as Tim felt a little tired he would want to go home. Tom put up with this for quite a while, even though he didn't understand why. One night, after they arrived at home, Tom confronted Tim and asked, "Why did we have to come home just because you got a little tired? What's wrong with you anyway?"

Tim immediately started to cry, and as he explained all the old feelings of being different and being the target of cruel name-calling, his own feelings of inadequacy came tumbling out. He had to leave the parties early because he believed that if his friends saw his eyes crossing he would be regarded as ugly and be rejected again. Yes, he even thought that Tom would no longer love him. Being the wonderful person he was, Tom reassured Tim that the eye problem did not matter, that he would always love him.

Palm Springs was a favorite vacation place, and they would go there at a moment's notice. Some of the best times were not planned, just spontaneous. Las Vegas was part of their travel itinerary also. Just as most of us have to do, they would decide on an amount of money they could afford to lose at gambling, and when that was gone they would quit. It worked that way most of the time, but occasionally Tom would get carried away and then he had to deal with an angry partner.

During their relationship they made a trip to Hawaii, the beautiful place where Tom had lived and where his grandparents lived until their deaths.

Many friends played a big part in their social life. Sometimes it was an unplanned get-together, a formal dinner, or a big party or celebration.

During the week they would come home from work very stressed out and relax with a drink or two. Then they would fix dinner, eat, do the dishes, watch a little television and go to bed. On the weekend, they cleaned house, shopped for groceries, took care of their flowers, washed their cars, and perhaps sat in the sun for a little while. Maybe someone would have something a little special going on so they would be invited out, or maybe they would have friends in. Once in a while they would go out to a bar, mostly for the social aspect of it. Sounds very normal like the things we all do except the couple consists of two young men rather than a man and woman. When a homosexual couple make a long-term commitment and settle down to make a home, it is very much like the home they grew up in.

# TWELVE

# Down Into The Valley

## North Detroit Street

At the end of April, 1985, they were getting ready to move into one unit of a duplex on North Detroit in West Hollywood. They had started packing. For quite a while Tim had been having nuisance illnesses which lasted longer than they should have. He had enlarged lymph glands, and a few pale brown spots were appearing across his chest and shoulders. It was probably fear and denial, but Tim did not go to the doctor. Tom begged Tim to make an appointment and to see what the problem really was. So Tim gave in and went to see if his fears would be confirmed.

There was no question; the diagnosis was Kaposi Sarcoma, the cancer associated with AIDS. After his worst fears were confirmed, Tim came home, took all the tranquilizers in the house and drank enough Vodka to put him out of his misery. I think he wanted it to be permanent, but it turned out to be only temporary. The truth was very painful, particularly for a seemingly healthy, twenty-five-year-old man who had a stable loving relationship, a career with a future and supposedly his whole life ahead. To suddenly be told he was going to die, probably within next two years, was just too much to accept with grace.

As they were supposed to move the next day, Tom spent the whole night sitting among their possessions packing and crying. It was a time of nightmares as the fabric of their life together was beginning to unravel.

**California Trip: Tim, Dave and Mike**

# THIRTEEN

## Shadows Of Death

### The Roller Coaster Ride Begins—
### Graduation Day

May 28, 1985, was the day I graduated from college with a degree in elementary education. It was a beautiful day in Lindsborg, Kansas, and I was so happy because all of my family was home. It was good to have loved ones around as I embarked on a new phase of my life.

Tim and Tom had come the week before and Tim wasn't feeling well. However, he looked so healthy I tried not to worry, but deep in my heart I was apprehensive. The boys were glad to be out of the big city rat race and had been enjoying the quaintness and peace of our unique Swedish community.

One day I was rubbing Tim's neck, and the lymph gland that had always been enlarged was even more so. Still I put it aside because this was my time, a celebration of my achievements. Tim was very proud of his mother.

Graduation day began with my brother, Shannon, and his wife, Patsy, arriving with my mother from Minnesota. Dave and I attended the breakfast Bethany College had for their graduates, and by the time we got home everyone was prepared for the family picture that was scheduled to be taken. Little did I know how much that picture was to mean to me because it would be the last one that included Tim. Yes, the family circle was soon to be broken.

We all gathered in the living room: Dave and I, my mother, Pam with her husband Doug and their little ones, Sean and Colleen; Mike and his wife Sherri and their baby Joshua, with Tim and Tom completing the family, because we loved Tom as a son. The picture was taken and a moment of time was frozen in an image forever.

Reservations for dinner had been made at a local restaurant. I noticed that Tim ordered only a salad, which he didn't finish. He seemed very reserved, and the only other word to describe his behavior is careful.

At 3:00 P.M. the graduation ceremony began. I was very proud and happy as I crossed the stage and got my diploma as the most senior person in the senior class.

After the ceremonies were over, there was to be an open house at my home. Many people came to wish me well and for food and fellowship. The whole family was around, but Tim stayed upstairs, saying he wasn't feeling well. My heart was very heavy with concern by this time. In the middle of my party I went upstairs and found Tim in the back bedroom, staring out of the window. "Tim, what is wrong?" I asked. He looked at me with tears in his eyes and told me to go downstairs, he didn't want to spoil my party. I looked at him and asked, "Is it AIDS?" He said

"Yes," and I took him in my arms and we cried. I told him I loved him and then went downstairs to play out the charade of the happy graduate.

Later he showed me the light brown spots on his upper arms and chest which were the indicators of Kaposi Sarcoma, the cancer brought on by a non-functioning immune system. He told me he had been diagnosed a month earlier, the day before he and Tom were to move from Orange County to West Hollywood.

The question uppermost in my mind was, "Why does this have to happen to Tim? Hasn't he suffered enough in his short life time?" There were so many times that I had held this little boy in my arms and cried with him and tried to kiss the hurt away, right the wrongs and bind the wounds, but it was never quite enough.

While still in high school, Tim put these words on paper which revealed a deep feeling of melancholy. Although he was never abandoned, many are, and it seemed to be a premonition of the hopelessness he and so many are feeling at this time, the time of the AIDS plague.

*Tiny drops of rain spill across the wind-*
*shield to match the tears of lost love.*
*A baby cries in the cold for the warmth*
*of its mother.*
*A dog whines impatiently outside the*
*front door of a vacant apartment.*
*A women picks at any crumbs she can find*

81

*left in cupboard, while her children*
*cry for dinner.*
*A young man, shortly after discovering*
*success, lies abandoned in a hospital.*

*War continues*

*And the rain carries on ...*
*Carries on while the baby is lost in the slum*
*Carries on while the dog lies dead in a gutter*
*Carries on while the woman runs from her starv-*
*ing children to be stabbed in the alley*
*Carries on while the young man dies of leukemia*
*Carries on while I give the accelerator a harsh*
*push*

*And War Continues*

Tim Barbo

# FOURTEEN

# Christmas Past –
# Christmas Present

## No Christmas Future

Tim was a super salesman for Pacific Bell (Pacific Telesis), winning many awards over the years. By November of 1985 he began to have trouble dealing with the customers in the professional way that made him successful. Not functioning at maximum efficiency, he opted for disability, always thinking that this was just a temporary problem. In his heart he believed he would beat the virus some way and could return to work. His superiors told him the job would be waiting for him whenever he felt he could come back.

Because of the positive attitude of both Tim and Tom, they were asked to speak before many groups of AIDS patients and others. Most of this was arranged through APLA (Aids Project Los Angeles). This is a wonderful organization that helps the victims of this disease with any problems they may have. They have experts to deal with personal problems, unemployment, finding places to live, legal rights, finding help (attendants and nurses), nursing services, food and the staff offers general support.

Tim's condition was up and down with various infections and viruses until December when he became so ill that they, he and Tom, asked me to come out and stay awhile. Up to this point Tim had been able to keep the house clean and do the cooking. Now he couldn't cope with the simplest household chores, so the whole burden fell on Tom. The difficulty of managing a high pressure job, keeping up the household and caring for Tim was overwhelming. I can truly say, "I have seen love," because through all of this, Tom remained very kind and loving toward Tim.

At that point I was truly thankful that I had not been able to get a full-time teaching position. I was substitute teaching and had no continuing responsibility to the school system, so I was available for Tim and Tom. As I look back I believe that it was supposed to be that way and that God had allowed my unemployment for a higher purpose.

## My First "Care for Tim" Trip

In the middle of December, 1985, I flew into LAX, a place with which I was to become very familiar in the next year. The boys' friend, Everett, was to meet me and bring me to their house. He had no trouble finding me, so we collected my bags and started off to the little house on North Detroit. I had no idea it would truly be a home to me for half of the next year. The roller coaster ride had truly begun.

Tim was extremely ill at this time, and when I walked in the door and saw him lying on the sofa, I went to him. We hugged, and I held him as I promised that he would get better and that he would be up and around again. That was a very foolish promise to make, but it proved to be true.

Getting acclimated to Los Angeles after living in Lindsborg (population 3,000) was quite a culture shock. The first errand they sent me on was to a local grocery store to do the weekly shopping. I think the number of people in the grocery store was equal to half the population of Lindsborg, and they were vicious with their carts. I found that the best way to shop was to park my cart at the end of the aisle, collect the items needed and bring them to the cart. Well, after that first outing I knew why Tom assigned that little task to me, and I also suspected that I was stuck with it. The experience was survival of the fittest, but I managed.

The biggest problem that Tim was going to face was just beginning. What had been light brown spots were getting darker and becoming more apparent. A fistula in the rectal area was causing extreme discomfort. It was the cancer invading the bowel that would be the biggest contributor to his death.

With some tender loving care from mom, along with three nourishing and fattening meals each day, Tim did slowly improve. Part of the time he could drive to the doctor's office or hospital which was very helpful as I could ride along, check out the route taken and get acclimated to the traffic.

Christmas for me would be very different this year.

I reflected on some of the Christmases past, from the time Tim was a tiny baby until now.

When we had lived in Minnesota, close to family, we would always spend Christmas Eve with Grandma and Grandpa Barbo and Christmas Day with Grandma and Grandpa Foote. All of the families would be there, and all of our children remembered these times and treasured them. Over the years there were far too few family holidays.

They remembered Grandma Barbo's silver tinsel tree and they knew there would be lutfisk, meat balls, roast pork for the meat courses and mushy applesauce for desert at dinner time.

Love and loved ones were in abundance at my parents' home, and my children remembered that when the din from the basement became too great, my father's booming voice would echo through the house, "What are you kids doing down there anyway?" There was stunned quiet ... but only for a few minutes.

Dave and I had purchased some property in Florida one year while we lived in Milwaukee. The four Christmases following that, we spent in Florida in kind of a family reunion with all of the other people who had purchased land at the same time. Every year brought the same families to the same motel, so we had good times there. Pam and Mike had friends their age and even though there were no children Tim's age, I know he enjoyed himself. In some way he was living on the edge of others' good times.

It sounds as if Tim had a black cloud over his head as he grew up and I think to some extent that is true because if any toy or other Christmas gift was broken, wouldn't work or was missing a part, it would be Tim's.

I still have Tim's Christmas stocking at home and use it for any of the grandchildren who spend Christmas with us.

AIDS Project Los Angeles was sponsoring a picnic in the park to help those with AIDS have some sense of holiday and festivity in their lives. This was an important event because there were so many who had nothing to do and nowhere to go at Christmas time.

I went with Tim and Tom to the building where the picnic was being held. The food, supplied by volunteers, was wonderful and there were gifts, mostly necessities of life, for anyone in need to take. Entertainment was also supplied to help these young men take their minds off the reality of the nightmare they were living.

There was a real effort to make this a viable party, but sadness pervaded the festivities because of the circumstances of these young lives. The love and care was apparent as the healthy one in each couple would help his partner get his food and sometimes even feed him. They would go to the gift selection area and choose the item or items that were the most needed. Tears came to my eyes and coursed down my cheeks as I watched and listened to these young men, who were mere shells of what they had been, join in the Christmas carols.

There were many tears that day. I am sure there were many Christmases past being remembered and many lost families mourned. **"Joy To The World,"** indeed! **"Hark The Herald Angels Sing,"** (Are these some of God's angels?) I would agree more with the carol **"Oh Come, Oh Come, Emmanuel,"** (Yes Come, Jesus) **"To Ransom Captive Israel,"** (Can these captives be another Israel?) **"Who Dwell In Lonely Exile Here,"** (Exiles from life, the new lepers,) **"Until The Son Of God Appears,"** (There will be a better place for them,) **"Rejoice, Rejoice."**

When the singing was over, we left. I wonder now how many of the seemingly healthy young men at the picnic have lost their loved ones and were back as the sick ones in 1986. How many will die before next Christmas?

Although Tim had been home for Thanksgiving two years before, it had been a long time since we had been together for Christmas. He had chosen to be with Tom and their friends, which was right and good because his home was with them. Dave and I had either spent Christmas by ourselves, or with the families of our other two children. We would alternate with the other side of each family, the in-laws, because they too had to be considered. This was the natural order of things as children become independent and must live their own lives.

Tom's mother and father, Connie and Phil, had invited us to spend Christmas with them at their rented condominium in San Diego. The drive from Los Angeles to San Diego is quite long and proved to be very painful and strenuous for Tim. The fistula in the rectum gave him constant problems, so sitting was very difficult and he was exhausted by the time we reached the house.

When I met Connie, I knew immediately that she was a kind and loving person. As I talked to Phil, I sensed that he was a converted "Archie Bunker" personality, and how wonderful it was to see the love and care he showed to both Tom and Tim.

Tim covered up his pain and put on a good front while we participated in the conversation and Christmas Eve dinner with Tom's family.

Tommy teased to open gifts on Christmas Eve, so we were allowed to open one gift that night. Tim was very anxious that I open one particular gift. I was a little puzzled because it had come in the mail from Pam in Denver. What a wonderful surprise. It was a mother's ring with a stone representing each of my children's birthdays. They had decided together to get me this one precious gift, and I felt so much love represented from each of my children.

Christmas morning came and Tim had been refreshed by the night's rest. No night was without its problems now, but it was as good as could be expected. We were to have an early dinner on Christmas Day, so Connie and I were in the kitchen preparing the meal. We were discussing Tom's and Tim's relationship. We both felt the same way because we loved these wonderful young men; they were our children. We acknowledged that this life style is not what we would have chosen for our boys, but if this is the way it had to be, we were glad they had found each other.

Dinner found us around the dining room table toasting each other, the new year and life. Earlier everyone had received beautiful gifts and Tim's were no different from anyone else's. This seemed to affirm the idea that he would go on with his life, that the disease would pass. Oh, how much each one of us wanted to believe that.

After dinner Tom, his folks and I went out to look at some property they had purchased. Tim was very tired, so he stayed home and slept, preparing for the long ride home.

Between Christmas and New Year's, a party was held at Tim's and Tom's house. Many of their friends came, everyone bringing something to eat and drink, but most importantly they brought love and support to Tim and Tom. What wonderful, intelligent and interesting people—to know them is to love them—and to know them expands my view as to what wonderful, diverse people God chose to complete our experience in this life.

**"The Sound of Music"**

91

**Junior High Years — Seeking Acceptance**

# FIFTEEN

# "Many Are Called, But Few Are Chosen"

## Futility and Frustration

The serious side of life at this time was Tim's futility in dealing with the disease, and both of us trying to get some medical help for him. Frustration was with us all the time as we tried everything to get on a protocol (experimental course of treatment.)

The AIDS virus was never found in Tim's blood, although U.S.C. and U.C.L.A. took many cultures. At that time the virus had to be found in order to truly say Tim had AIDS, and the proof had to be there before any doctor would include him in a protocol.

I accompanied Tim to a meeting at U.S.C. where Dr. Alexandra Levine, oncologist, and Dr. Sylvia Fermenti, radiation oncologist, (both very committed to AIDS research) were going to dialogue with AIDS patients. This gave me a look at the scope and harsh realities of living with AIDS as there were people there at various stages of the disease. Some had been driven there by their partners, but many had women friends who were caring for them. There was no hesitation on the part of these young men to voice their fears and frustrations.

Some were food handlers and hospital workers with questions about what precautions they should take, and what their rights were. Questions about the latest medications and criteria to obtain access to them. Worries about dealing with the families on the contagion issue. One young man was now being frozen out of his family because they thought the virus might change and they would get it.

Dr. Levine's response to that was, "Yes, the virus can change, but the way you catch it doesn't. It won't be you in casual contact with other people or the little kids in school who have the virus who will spread it. It will be irresponsible people, including moms and dads, carrying on promiscuously with everyone and anyone who will propagate this disease."

Tim expressed his frustration about the fact that no matter how many blood samples were taken from him to culture, the virus had never shown up, yet his general condition was deteriorating.

Dr. Levine and Dr. Fermenti truly seemed interested in this phenomenon and asked us to stay later, after the meeting. They talked with Tim at length, got the history of his disease and told us to come to the hospital the next day so they could take blood for more extensive tests. Tim and I were very excited and we were very impressed with these two doctors. They really seem to care. "Thank You, God, a ray of hope."

Sometimes patients can become just a number and not a human being as the disease spreads. I compare the whole process to a cattle call in the theatre. "Many are called but few are chosen." In the theatre there are criteria people must meet for any given part. The majority are rejected only to come back and try again for another role.

With AIDS at that time, the patient had to meet certain criteria to get any help with the disease. It wasn't enough that the person was very ill and blood tests had shown he had been exposed to the virus, the AIDS virus itself must show up in a culture of the patient's blood. Other determinations were: What opportunistic diseases the patient had experienced, it couldn't have been too many. What stage of the disease the patient was in. What medications the patient was on. How sick was the patient. So with all these and many more considerations, many are called to have the disease, but few are chosen to be able to do anything about it. This is not for a role or a part, this is for life, and there may not be a chance to try again.

Tim and I made the trip to the hospital the next day. We were ushered into the doctor's office almost immediately. As the staff were drawing the blood we felt so hopeful that there might be an opportunity to do something—anything—to fight this disease. Win or lose, it would be better than the frustration of being offered nothing. Under any circumstances a waiting period would be required before the hospital would have any results from all the tests taken.

Quite some time elapsed as we anxiously awaited

word from Dr. Levine. When a report was given it seemed that everything was inconclusive. Although there were promises that something might be available, we felt totally discouraged. It seemed we would have to fight the disease ourselves with diet, vitamins, exercise, meditation, positive thinking, and prayer. I am glad we could still hope and that we were not aware how flimsy these weapons were in the battle against this disease. The body cannot fight back at all as the whole immune system is broken down and cannot be repaired.

# SIXTEEN

## And Life Goes On

### Hollywood

Tim was well enough to be left alone, so in order to keep my sanity and perspective on life I sometimes would go shopping. Melrose Avenue was only two blocks from the house, so I would go down to this extremely bizarre street and watch people. It is an education in the diversity of people. Sometimes dressed in my blue jeans and cowboy boots (very Kansas), I felt like someone from another planet.

There were many Punkers, young people who have to be so different from the mainstream and yet alike among themselves. I believe they were making a statement about who they were without having found out themselves. Maybe it is a reflection of the futility of life as they interpret it.

The street people (and there are many of them) are another study in futility. Maybe they have no one who cares because their needs are very evident, but it is also evident that those needs are not being met. People walk down the street, talking to themselves and I wonder, is there anyone to answer? Is the only person they have, themselves, or some imaginary being?

There was a middle-aged man who was filthy dirty, and it appeared that he lived in a doorway next to the doughnut shop on Melrose. He would come into the shop for coffee, confiscate a lot of cream and sugar and sit down in his doorway to drink it. Maybe that was all he had.

Another favorite spot was Beverly Center, a shopping center for those a bit more affluent than the average American. The whole eighth floor is dedicated to eating and the movies, so I would get some coffee and usually a muffin and find a table in the middle of the mall where I would sit and eat. Most of the time it was so crowded that I would end up at a table with other people. Sometimes a great conversation would take place, and other times there was deathly silence. Many times I felt like a minority. It seemed that English was not always the first language spoken by those around me. Sometimes on Saturdays when Tom was home, I would go to a movie for diversion. These places were my refuge from reality during the next year.

Observing Tim, I was astounded by his knowledge of the disease and the medications he must take for every infection, virus or parasite. He really listened to his body and had become an expert in juggling his medication. He had to become even more of an expert to live through and endure the next few months.

The cancer was spreading. The innocent-appearing

brown spots were rapidly becoming voracious leprous-like tumors that seem to be devouring the surface of Tim's skin. We knew that for every lesion on the outside, there were many more on the inside. He was having extreme rectal-bowel problems, but there was still no word from U.S.C. As a whole Tim's health was better, and he had put on some weight. Sometimes he felt well enough to go out, and we could do some things together.

We had some wonderful times. We took walks in Griffith Park, which is widely used and has well-worn paths, and then we found a wonderful little out-of-the way park that very few people knew about. It was there we would sit in the sun and talk about whatever was important to Tim at that time. We discussed books, philosophy, diet, faith and death. It was also a time when we could talk about the past and the good or bad things about his life and our life together as a family.

Occasionally we would go to a restaurant and eat. He took me to some delightful places, and we really did enjoy each other's company.

## Welcome to L.A.

Los Angeles proved to be a very expensive place for me. One morning I woke up with a sore throat, and not wanting to pass anything on to Tim, I looked through the yellow pages, called and made an appointment with a doctor nearby. I drove to the clinic and parked my car on the street in an area marked off for parking. There were other cars parked there too. The doctor cost me $45, which I had to put on my VISA because I was running out of cash. When I came out my car was gone, so I walked to the middle of the block where there was a sign and found out that it said, "No Parking after 4:00 P.M." I found out the hard way that LaBrea was a busy throughway by having my car towed away.

I walked to the drugstore "Thrifty" (which is a story in itself) and after an hour paid $17 for my prescription. Then I walked home and Tom called the police to find out where my car was. He was going to go with me to pick up the car, but because it was registered in Tim's name he had to get out of his sick bed and go with us. For a mere $60 I could have the car back, but as the hour had just changed I talked him down to $48. The final frustration was paying the parking ticket for $28. Welcome to L.A.

As I went on cooking, cleaning and playing chauffeur day after day, I knew Tim was getting well enough so that I didn't need to be there all the time. So I told him and Tom to tell me when it was time to leave.

Tim still had some bad days, so I was to stay a little longer. Although having me around all the time did cause some problems, I felt that we got along very well. It was also a relief for Tom not to have to come home and cook, and simply knowing that I was there for Tim relieved his stress.

## Jose Eber's

Before I was to leave, they wanted to give me a special treat. One Saturday they sent me to Jose Eber's Beauty Salon with $200 and an order to live it up. I had an appointment with Jose for a consultation during which he told the stylist his ideas about cut, color and style. I was then sent to the shampoo room. Everyone in the shop has a specialty.

Coming out of the shampoo area with my hair dripping wet and towel wrapped around my head, I was pleasantly surprised to find Gary Collins in my stylist's chair getting a haircut. Some weeks before I had tried to get tickets for his show, "Hour Magazine," and was unsuccessful because they cater to groups, and it seemed they were all booked up for quite some time.

As he stood up, I said, "Gary Collins?" He said, "Yes." So I shook his hand, introduced myself and proceeded to tell him about not being able to get in to see his show. He took out a card, wrote down a name and telephone number, and told me to tell this person that Gary had requested a ticket for me. Needless to say, I was very pleased. What a nice man.

I enjoyed being pampered and my hair was cut, colored, curled, brushed and styled. Including parking, that trip cost $175 but I must admit I looked very chic, like I belonged in Los Angeles.

The boys were so pleased that they wanted to show me off, so they made dinner reservations for us, along with their best friend, Jeff. The restaurant was very crowded and filled with smoke. We had a long wait for our table, and I could see Tim getting sicker by the minute. He became so ill that he asked Tom to call a cab for him, and he went home. I had a wonderful time with Jeff and Tom but couldn't get Tim off my mind. By the nature of his illness, he had to be left out again.

## Hour Magazine

On Monday I called "Hour Magazine" for the ticket and was told to simply give my name to the parking attendant and to the people at the studio. I felt very special as I parked the little green Fiesta in the parking lot of the stars and was seated in front row where I watched the preparation for the show.

I had my new hairdo, was very dressed up, but because my watch had quit working, was wearing a Mickey Mouse watch Tim had given me. When a live audience is involved, there is what I call a warmup man who before the show gets everyone in a jovial mood and enthusiastic. He wandered through the crowd getting acquainted, asking questions and making jokes.

When he asked if anyone had seen any stars, I raised my hand and he spotted Mickey Mouse. He came over to me, turned to the audience and said, "Believe it or not, here we have a lady all dressed up and wearing a Micky Mouse watch. That requires an explanation." I said, "I am in Hollywood, need I say more?" I told him my name, where I was from and that I had met Gary Collins at Jose Eber's a few days before. At this point Gary looked over at me and said, "My word, it is you." Then he said to the audience, "She looks good today; the last time I saw her she looked like a drowned puppy." The show started and it was extremely interesting to see how it was put together. It had been a good day.

The next Sunday the boys dressed up and went out to a bar together. It was the first time in a long time that Tim was strong enough to do this. He wanted to do something to please Tom even if he didn't feel as well as he led us to believe. He looked very handsome, almost his old self. It was time for me to think about going home. Home, where was my real home, where did I belong?

## Catalina

Since Tim was temporarily on the mend, it was a good time for Dave to come out and visit. Tim and Tom thought it would be pleasant for all of us to spend a day on the island of Catalina, so one sunny morning we boarded the boat that would take us the short distance between the island and the mainland. Tim slept on the bench that ran the length of the boat while the rest of us enjoyed the beautiful morning. When we reached Catalina we wandered along the shore and among the beach-front businesses and then found a comfortable little sidewalk cafe and ordered lunch. It was a lazy day, so we took our time. Later Tim and Dave explored more of the beach area while Tom and I visited every garage sale we could find. Soon it was time for the last boat to leave, so we said goodbye to this beautiful island and I thanked God for another good day.

Dave and I got back to Lindsborg the first part of February and immediately got involved in local activities. Our community had presented the Messiah at Easter for 104 years and the 400-voice choir was in rehearsal every Tuesday and Sunday until Holy Week. It was wonderful to participate in the event and it felt good to do something for myself again, to be part of things. No matter how great the pain, life goes on. As I functioned daily within my house and my town, life was the same, but there was always a heaviness in my heart knowing what Tim's prognosis was.

Maybe he will get better; maybe a cure will be found. Inside there is a little voice telling me that it is foolish to believe this, but hope is all I have. To look at the statistics is really too painful right now. He did get better this time, didn't he? Perhaps it's a shadow of things to come. If only he didn't have the cancer my hope would be greater.

**Minnesota: Everyone hugged Tim and Tom,
what Love is all about**

# SEVENTEEN

# Goodbye – An Affirmation Of Love

## Minnesota Visit

Our phone bills were tremendous, but this was a small price to pay for keeping in touch, for just hearing his voice. He had been in the hospital off and on as small problems became big ones for him. His blood count would go so low that he had to go in for regular blood transfusions, but he was still fighting with everything within him. At this time Tim was very self-conscious about his appearance. As the lesions increased in number and were turning a dark color, he sought out a dermatologist to administer radiation to the individual lesions, particularly those on his hands. It was only a temporary solution to the cosmetic problem. It was not successful.

We were hopeful that we would get some word from Dr. Levine at U.S.C., but as the weeks passed it seemed as though Tim had fallen through the cracks once more. He was really on his own with the enemy. Everyone around him supported, encouraged and loved him, which was good for the spirit and soul, but the disease that had invaded his body needed a potent adversary such as a medical breakthrough or a miracle from God. Tim was taking a day at a time but couldn't obtain the weapons to get a stay of execution.

Tim was reading Norman Cousin's book, **"The Anatomy of An Illness"** and was concentrating on maintaining a healthy diet in order to get the proper nutrients. He was trying to take large doses of vitamin C by mouth, but his system couldn't tolerate the amounts suggested in the book. Doctors were very hesitant about large doses by infusion, so that too was taken away from Tim.

My mother is a wonderful woman and she loved Tim very much. Every time I talked to her on the phone it seemed as though she had heard about some new treatment or medication that was coming out or was currently being tested. She wrote down everything she heard and passed it on to Tim and me. She tried so hard to help.

Pam expressed Tim's need to her congregation and they prayed for him. Our congregation was praying, even though they didn't know the exact illness Tim was suffering from. I only said that it was cancer, for AIDS was not an acceptable disease to be dying from and I was not totally out of the closet yet. I was very vulnerable and was not ready to deal with judgmental people.

God was taking his time squeezing me out of my little box of narrow thinking and conformity, like someone squeezing toothpaste from a tube. Going through dark times has been compared to peeling an onion; it makes one cry but as each layer of protection is stripped off a new more vulnerable surface appears. Perhaps it is more like cutting a diamond, in that much of the rough and ugly rock must be chipped away before something beautiful, strong and valuable appears.

As the weeks passed, Tim had more infections and fevers. Blood transfusions were regularly needed, and he was losing weight again. It seemed as though some of his body systems were beginning to close down, so in May of 1986 Tim and Tom decided to fly to Minnesota to visit family and to say goodbye. Grandma's house was the closest thing to a home place Tim had because of all our moves. They asked me to be there, thinking it would be easier for everyone concerned.

I decided that I should go before Tim and Tom to provide a buffer and to prepare everyone. My mother and sister were the only ones with whom I had shared Tim's homosexuality and his AIDS diagnosis. My brother, Shannon and his wife Pat, must have guessed that Tim was gay when at my graduation we included Tom in the family picture, but they never said anything and neither did I.

Now was the time when it had to be told. I truly believe that God had a hand in arranging the meeting to make things easier for me. I didn't have to seek my brothers out or invite them over to mother's house, because one morning they came over together to have coffee with Mom and me.

Tim had told me to tell everyone that he would be at Grandma's house and those who could handle the situation to come and visit him. If there were those who couldn't, he would understand. My brothers reacted with the typical love and caring that is expressed so easily in my family. They started to cry, came over and hugged me and reassured me that Tim and Tom would be welcome in their homes. Their wives could have objected, but they reacted in the same loving way. "Thank You, God for such a wonderful family."

When the boys arrived, Tim was very tired and worn out. He had to wear slippers because of a painful lesion on his toe. He spent most of the day on the davenport, and went upstairs to bed very early.

The next day was party time. We were invited to my brother Shannon's home for dinner and the whole clan was there—cousins, aunts, uncles, in-laws, children and babies. No one seemed to be afraid of Tim as there was a lot of hugging and close contact. Everyone had a wonderful time, and Tim even had a good appetite for dinner. The whole family loved Tom, but then there isn't much not to love.

My brother Bud's family was just getting over the flu and asked if we would drive over to their house. Those that were healthy enough would come out and talk with Tim by the car. (They didn't want to endanger Tim by exposing him to the flu.) We spent quite some time in conversation, and when it started to get cold and Tim was getting chilled, there were more hugs from the well ones in this family and then we went back to Mom's house.

While there, my sister and her family stopped by for a visit. Again there were hugs all around as they said goodbye. Tim must have felt very affirmed as a much-loved human being as he prepared to go back to L.A.

At Grandma's Tim slept quite a bit. His bowel problem was getting worse and he was becoming very thin. As tired as he was, there was one place Tim wanted to visit, the old Nicholas Cemetery. It dates back to the 1700's and much of my family is buried there. As we walked past all of the old stones of our ancestors from many generations back, I think it gave Tim a sense of being part of a continuum, a part of the grand scheme of life. It was so peaceful as we wandered through the cemetery reading the headstones. It gave us pause as we thought of those who had gone on before and brought us to focus on our own mortality. Tim felt encompassed by the love that was shown him by his family and comfortable with the idea that there would be those waiting for him as he made his crossing from this world to the next.

In a few days it was time for us to leave. The planes to Los Angeles and Wichita were leaving the same day so we started to the airport in the boys' rented car. Tim started driving but soon became so tired that he had to pull over and let Tom take over. (I think Tim was still trying to prove that he wasn't hopelessly ill.)

At the airport we had to wait awhile for the plane to L.A., and my flight to Wichita was even later. As we sat around it was evident that Tim was extremely ill. His fever had begun and he had trouble sitting up. At last they called the flight to L.A., and I was so glad that it was a direct flight.

As I hugged the boys and bade them goodbye I wondered if I would ever see Tim again and if I did, in what condition? I marvel at the loving care and enduring spirit Tom expresses for Tim. As Tim, this tall skeletal figure, leaned against Tom while they boarded the plane, truly again I was seeing love.

Later as I boarded my plane, I tried to envision how it must be for Tom as he had committed himself to care for Tim and it was obviously becoming more of a burden everyday. "God, thank you for Tom." Thinking about what was ahead made me sad. I didn't want to face that yet, so I made light conversation with the gentlemen who sat next to me. (Part of my denial.)

**As "Faithful" in Pilgrim's Progress"**

# EIGHTEEN

## A Season Of Suffering

Dave and I had planned a trip to Europe some months before. As our departure time grew near we hoped and prayed that Tim's health would remain stable. We had purchased insurance, so if an emergency came up we were ready to scrap our plans and come home.

Every phone conversation with Tim was full of confidence as he led us to believe that he was holding his own and that he was having a better period in his struggle with the disease. We were happy when we left for Europe.

It was a wonderful trip and Dave and I needed the time away. We sent postcards to all of our family from every city we visited. When we phoned Tim, he was always cheerful and sounded full of hope.

In Tim's life was a young man whom I called his spiritual advisor, Steve Kant. Steve had been of great help to Tim for a long time. They could talk about God, love, relationships, philosophy, Christ, life and death. Steve's partner, Max, was also dying from AIDS. While we were away, Steve spent even more time with Tim which was of great comfort to Tom, Dave and me.

We felt good when we came home; as far as we knew Tim seemed to be doing very well. This illusion was to be shattered as soon as we called California. Within three days I was on my way to Los Angeles.

## July 1986

There was no one to pick me up at LAX this time so I found the Hollywood Super Shuttle, and with fear as to how I would find Tim, gave the driver the address of my home away from home. Riding on the shuttle with me was a young black woman, a musician, who had been offered a chance to get into the big time of music. She was extremely excited about starting her new life in L.A. She was probably about the same age as Tim, and as I sat there I thought, how ironic that she is starting life fresh and new while Tim is almost at the finish line.

After a half-hour drive we arrived at the house. The driver got my bags and helped me out of the van. I tipped him and started walking to the door.

As I opened the door Tim said, "Hi Mom." He was lying on the sofa and made an effort to get up. I went over and hugged him. We both had tears in our eyes. He was glad I was there. He was so thin that I could feel his bones through his shirt. The lesions had increased many fold. His temperature was elevated, and he told me the fevers were everyday occurrences now. The fistula in his rectum was always draining and caused extreme pain.

I looked at him and thought, "What can I do for you this time, my Timothy? Oh, help me, God!" He wouldn't get better this time, although I tried everything to nourish him, to put some weight on him, and to prod his body into fighting back.

After dinner that evening a group of AIDS patients and their partners were to meet at Tim's and Tom's house. It had become somewhat depressing because there were no couples in that group that had been there when Tim and Tom joined. One of every couple that had composed the original group had died. However, everyone seemed to agree that the mutual support was good therapy.

No one outside the group was invited to attend, so I went to my bedroom and spent the evening watching a movie on TV. It was about a teenager dying of cancer. How appropriate.

Later, sharing what went on in the group, the boys told me about a young man who was in the hospital and was expected to die soon. He experienced a vision of all his loved ones who had passed from this life, standing around his bed. It made him unafraid of death. Somehow that gave Tim reassurance and a feeling of peace. He was very out of it mentally that evening, and he spent all of the meeting time on the floor with his head in Tom's lap. In the morning he told us that he really didn't think he would wake up, and, in some ways I think he wished he hadn't.

# Madrigal Singers — Arapahoe High School,

**Miss Dillon, director**

# NINETEEN

# Is There Something Else For Tim To Do?

## Spiritual Awareness

The next day Steve came over for one of his sessions with Tim, and they requested that I stay. Tim lay on the davenport while Steve and I pulled chairs up close so that we could talk and pray without causing Tim any undue stress. We reminisced and talked about how valuable family and friends are at all times in our lives and particularly at the point of transition. Then Tim asked that we all pray that he might die at that moment. He really didn't want to be in this world as he was.

With tears in our eyes each of us prayed to that end. After fifteen or twenty minutes Tim opened his eyes and decided that as long as God hadn't taken him, there must be something else for him to do.

Tim was getting thinner and was always extremely

tired. We realized that there was probably more than just an infected fistula causing his problems. Whatever it was, it caused some type of bowel blockage.

## Philosophical Decisions

Tim made regular visits to his personal physician, Dr. Steve Knight. Dr. Knight is a man of extraordinary kindness and caring. The people in his office were great, and they all seemed to care a great deal about Tim. There were always friendly hellos and loving hugs.

He had an appointment to see Dr. Knight that afternoon, so he took a shower and changed clothes. Tim had lost all self-consciousness and wore short-sleeved shirt and shorts which did not cover his ugly lesions. The fistula dripped infection and at times showed through his shorts. When I remarked about it, he simply shrugged his shoulders and said that it was out of his control.

Each visit began with weighing in, which showed us if Tim was really in trouble or in a state of holding. As soon as he was in the examining room he would have to lie down on the examining table so he could rest. I think he must have had all the holes in the ceiling tile counted because he had been there so many times.

After examining Tim, Dr. Knight took me into his office. I asked why Tim was still losing weight when he was eating so well. He said that the food was not being fully utilized by Tim's body and that the cancer had a life of its own and was sapping Tim's energy.

Dr. Knight had become very attached to Tim, and I admired him very much for the kind of person he was and for how he was managing Tim's illness. He began to explain that the cancer was undoubtedly causing the bowel obstruction and that it would probably be the obstruction that would in some way cause Tim's death. There was nothing that could be done.

By this time the tears were running down his face as he took a tissue and handed one to me. As we both sat there trying to hold back the tears, I asked him about chemotherapy and approximately how long Tim had. He believed that chemo would only make Tim's life more unbearable, and being the compassionate person he was he didn't recommend it. In fact, he thought Tim might have only two to three weeks left and probably less if he started chemo. (This was only one of the times Tim proved the doctors wrong.) He talked about quality of life versus quantity and Tim having to make philosophical decisions about his life and death. I told him that I would not try to influence Tim for or against chemo, that he would have to decide for himself.

We returned to the examining room, and Dr. Knight told Tim what he had told me. Tim had one of those philosophical decisions to make immediately—he needed a blood transfusion which would extend his life a little longer. This choice was an easy one for Tim; he would go for it.

# High School Senior

# TWENTY

# At The End Of Hope

## Medical Questions

As the weight loss, the fever and rectal/bowel problems got worse, Tim had reached the end of his hope. One day he began to feel anger at the system and wrote a letter to Dr. Levine. He told her how hopeful he had been in February when he was supposedly re-evaluated and had thought there might be some help from somewhere. However, since it had been months without any word he concluded that he had fallen through the cracks again or was lost in the red tape associated with getting any information about any protocol that might be appropriate. He wrote that she was his last chance for any help as the cancer was spreading rapidly.

She called him as soon as she received his letter. He made an appointment for the next day so his present condition could be evaluated. We had to go to the AIDS Clinic associated with U.S.C., which wasn't as pleasant as the day hospital at Norris Cancer Hospital (also affiliated

119

with U.S.C.)

The first hassle at the hospital was finding a parking place. Finally I pulled up to the entrance to let Tim out, hoping he would be able to cope while I went to find a place to park (and of course I had to pay).

When I entered the hospital, Tim was sitting in a general waiting area. By looking at him, I knew he would not be able to sit there much longer, so we went upstairs to the clinic immediately. He had not been there before, so there was a great deal of paperwork. This was a classic case of hurry-up and wait. While this was going on, we had to sit on some very uncomfortable wooden benches. By this time Tim was so ill that he was lying down on the bench and I was getting extremely angry. I asked the admitting person if there was a bed available because Tim would end up on the floor if he had to wait much longer.

An intern came out and took Tim into a room in the back of the admitting area while I helped finish the paperwork. When I went to join him I found him sitting in a recliner, which was more comfortable than the bench, but he really needed a bed.

Dr. Levine came into the room and chatted with Tim. She is wonderful at making patients feel good, and she does command their confidence. She asked him exactly what had been going on, how he felt physically and how he was doing emotionally. She commented on how much worse he looked than when she saw him last, but that in her opinion he didn't look as if he were dying. In my private thoughts I disagreed with her.

At this point we were introduced to Dr. Mark Rarick,

who would be Tim's doctor of record from then on. I left the room while Dr. Rarick thoroughly examined Tim. While I was out in the hall, I met another mother who was just beginning this lonely journey with her son. It would be more difficult for her as she was alone, and her son was younger, had no partner and little insurance.

After the examination Drs. Levine and Rarick agreed that it was time for chemotherapy. They wanted to start it that day, but Tim was exhausted and he needed some time to think and talk to Tom about it, so he asked if he could come back the next day. Dr. Rarick agreed saying that everything would be ready, that he would not have to wait as a bed would be available and the chemicals would be mixed and ready. The procedure would be done in the Day Hospital at Norris.

With everything settled, Tim sat in the waiting room while I went to get the car. An aide had helped Tim into a wheel chair so when I pulled up to the curb, Tim was waiting for me. He slept all the way home. In the evening Tom and Tim discussed the situation at length and agreed that it probably was the last hope.

## First Chemotherapy

The next day he was to go immediately to the Day Hospital. Everything was not in readiness; there were no beds available, so he had to sit in a recliner for awhile. He became so weak that they gave him the first available bed, even though there were others before him.

First, blood had to be taken for evaluation to determine whether or not his system could endure the chemo. When it was ascertained that it could, they had to mix the chemicals which was a long drawn-out process. They wouldn't mix chemicals early because if the patient didn't show up or wasn't in condition to receive chemo the mixture would be wasted. They were mixing three chemicals for Tim this time, two of which have few side effects, but the third could be quite toxic.

While we waited I went and got snacks for us and lots of water for Tim. At last everything was ready and the treatment began. After it was started it didn't take very long.

Many cancer patients came to the Day Hospital for treatment. The area consists of two large rooms, one with reclining chairs for those who are well enough to sit during chemotherapy while the other room has regular hospital beds set up in a ward situation with curtains that could be drawn around each bed.

The curtains were pulled when the doctors came in to examine the patients; otherwise we were one big group together (all of those receiving chemo and those few of us who were there to support them). Two small private rooms were off to one side of the ward. These were for the most critical patients. I didn't see another AIDS patient at any time we were there, at least no one whose lesions were visible.

As I sat with Tim while his treatment was being given, I talked with the others around me. As they looked at Tim, I wondered if they knew what those ugly lesions meant; I wondered if there was ever any fear.

On the way home Tim was more hungry than tired, which was unusual, and he asked me to stop at Arby's and to get him two roast beef sandwiches. When we got home, we sat down at the table and began to eat. He had finished one sandwich when the shakes began. He had extreme chills, his fever was spiking and he shook so hard he couldn't sit on the chair any longer, so he got down on the floor.

I didn't know what to do for him, but somehow I got him up and into bed where he shook so hard that the bed vibrated. I called Dr. Rarick and he told me to try to get the fever down, but that this reaction was not out of the ordinary.

I sponged him with water and alcohol, and after a period of time it passed and Tim went to sleep. Tom was getting extremely concerned as Tim's fever seemed to be with him all the time now. Infections of some kind were the norm, and the side effects of the chemo were very worrisome. Nights had gradually been getting worse, but it was nothing compared with what was to come.

Whenever Tim went to the hospital for anything, whether it was a blood transfusion, chemotherapy or some other treatment, he would be exhausted, yet voraciously hungry on the way home. Most of the time he was careful about what he ate, but on these occasions he threw caution to the wind. He craved junk food, so I would stop for an Arby's Roast Beef Sandwich or a Big Mac with fries and a shake.

I wanted him to eat so I didn't discourage him, but I was always a little apprehensive (with good cause, needless to say). After eating, he was always sick. His stomach wasn't used to being abused, but that was a minor problem compared to the way he suffered the next day.

Whatever went in had to come out, and this was agony as the obstruction seemed to get larger. The bathroom was to become the torture chamber of the house.

There seemed to be no more side effects from the chemo, and Tim actually felt fairly well for a few days. This was not to last, for in a short time the infection in the fistula flared up, and the medication for that made him extremely nauseous. He was losing weight even though he made valiant attempts to eat larger portions of food. His body could not consume enough to keep up with the unlimited appetite of the cancer.

# TWENTY-ONE

## There Is No Escape

### For Tim and Tom

Steve came for regular spiritual-support visits with Tim every week. One day Tim was feeling fairly well and was expecting Steve in the afternoon. Thinking this was going to be a regular 2-3 hour session, I made plans to leave the home for awhile. They were in the living room as I called out to them from the back door that I was leaving. As I drove off I felt secure in the fact that Tim was safe with his good friend. I was out for two hours and as I drove the car into the driveway I was happy to see that Tom was home.

As I entered the house I found Tom trying to get Tim to take some water. He was very angry at me for leaving. It seemed that Steve had only stayed for a short time and after he left Tim was feeling weak and sick. The drapes in the living room were still open with the sun streaming in and the room was very hot. Tim had been so weak he couldn't get up to shut the drapes so he became extremely overheated and dehydrated.

I closed the drapes and went outside to lower the shade, then I helped Tom get Tim into his bed and more comfortable. The fever was still high so Tom called Dr. Rarick. He told Tom to get Tim into the hospital; of course he preferred Norris, but at this point any hospital would do. Tim and Tom chose Sherman Oaks where Tim would be under Dr. Knight's care. At this time communication between Dr. Rarick and Dr. Knight opened up.

As Tom and I sat in the hospital waiting for Tim's fever to go down, I felt very guilty for allowing this to happen, and although Tom had apologized for his anger, I felt that he had been justified in feeling that way. "I am sorry, Tom."

## For Me

At this time my endurance was wearing down, and I felt that I needed some support from other people going through the same thing, people my own age. APLA gave me a time and place for a meeting of parents of AIDS victims. With great anticipation I got into the little green Fiesta and headed for the address on Santa Monica Boulevard. After finding a parking place and making my way up the flight of steps to the designated room, I found out that it wasn't a parents meeting at all, but a meeting for the newly- diagnosed AIDS patients.

## Or for Others

Well, when they and the counselors learned my situation, they wanted me to stay as a kind of surrogate parent. Each one got to tell their story. Some had their partners with them; some were alone. Three in the group were older than I was. One of these older gentlemen said that he had not been with anyone for four years, so this was a profound shock for him.

One young man had quit his job as soon as he knew that he was suffering from Kaposi Sarcoma. He knew his time on earth was limited, and so he set out to do the things he now had time for. He was fortunate in that the disease was not extremely aggressive at that time, and so he traveled all over Europe. That night it was apparent that his immune system was growing weaker and the cancer was taking its toll, so his plans to travel in the US would be limited.

Denial is the first stage of dealing with the diagnosis. Tony, a young Spanish-American, was denying that he would die because he was feeling so well at that time. After all, he had defeated pneumocystis pneumonia the first time around, so why wouldn't he be able to do it again. He had no significant other (no partner), so he had no one to talk to, no one to share his fears with except this group of strangers. He could not tell his family because, "If they knew I was gay they would have to disown me because of their interpretation of the Catholic faith which is so important to them." It was part of them and was the critical factor in their perception of how things should be; of what they could accept or would have to reject—even to the extreme of rejecting one of their own. Tony was not dealing with the situation in a realistic way. He would need more time.

Karl had lost his love some time ago. He had been serving as a volunteer with APLA since that time. Now as the disease was beginning its relentless onslaught in his body, he wondered how he would make it—alone.

Their questions to me were about how to tell their families, what reaction they might expect, and how to deal with rejection if indeed that was what they were faced with. I answered with the little wisdom that I had acquired with experience and gave them my telephone number, both in California and Kansas, in the event they had no one else to talk to.

When I returned home, Tim said, "I am sure they needed you there Mom, but it wasn't exactly what you needed tonight."

# TWENTY-TWO

## Oh God, Behold My Son

In between treatments there were usually a few days when Tim could function somewhat normally. One day we decided to go out for lunch. On the way to the restaurant Tim got very impatient with my driving; he said I was overly cautious. I ignored his criticism because I knew that it is just a defensive mechanism because he could no longer drive. My observations from watching Tim, my father, my grandfather and father-in-law were that when a man is stripped of the ability to drive it seems to make him feel impotent and helpless; that last freedom is gone.

We went to a family-style restaurant and although Tim looked ill, he had a long-sleeved shirt and long pants on so that the lesions didn't show, Tim ordered for us and it was obvious that he had thoroughly charmed the waitress with his smile and good humor.

I am ashamed to say that I was more self-conscious about Tim's appearance than he was. Another time we were going for a ride and I told him that if he had any thoughts about stopping for lunch to please dress appropriately. He said that he would probably be too tired for lunch, so we took off. He was dressed in a T-shirt and shorts.

It was about 11:30 A.M. and he suggested we stop somewhere to eat, but I said no, that I wasn't comfortable doing that. He became so angry that he accused me of being ashamed of him. I told him I wouldn't go because the cancer was so obvious that I didn't feel it was necessary to put ourselves in the position of being rejected by service being refused us. Also I said that if I had a skin disease, I wouldn't expect people to look at me while they were eating when all I had to do to cover it was to put on a long-sleeved shirt.

Again, I don't believe that he thought he looked all that bad and this was another "accept me as I am" move. At future times there was no discussion; he covered up.

Every day he would try to exercise. How sad it was to see this once handsome, now emaciated, spotted, worn-out hulk of a young man trying to rebuild his body with stretching, hand weights and even some aerobics done to Jane Fonda's tape.

Since there was no conventional treatment other than chemotherapy (which made him unfit for any new protocols) available to Tim, he tried holistic healing which involved prayer, meditation and imagery. One day we went to Venice Beach where his teacher in this healing endeavor lived. He went into her house and I walked the beach enjoying all the vendors and entertainers who live and work along this strip.

Then I walked down by the water, sat down in the warm sand, looked at the glorious sun shining over the restless waves, and listened to the birds and the swish of the water. I put my head in my hands and cried. There was such a sadness in me that I couldn't even pray. "Oh God, Behold my son!"

I found my way back to the house, sat down on the front steps and waited for Tim. In a few minutes he came out, put his hand on my shoulder and said, "I'm ready, Mom."

**Tim, his little green Fiesta, Palm Springs**

131

"California Dreaming," San Francisco

# TWENTY-THREE

## Letting Go

### Good Times

There were still some fairly good times to come. Tim and Tom took me to the Japanese restaurant where they had celebrated their fifth anniversary the year before. It was a beautiful evening, and we sat on the terrace over-looking the city. Tim was feeling as well as he ever did these days, and he and Tom were reminiscing about the good time they had last year with champagne and a large dinner. Now Tim could eat very little and although he wasn't supposed to drink at all, he took enough champagne to toast to the hope of better days ahead. We had a wonderful dinner, a very loving time together and then took a short walk in the Japanese Gardens. I believe Tim was pushing himself to the limit so that Tom and I would have a good evening.

Whenever Tim felt fairly well, Tom would encourage him to get away from the house. One of those times was a beautiful, sunny Sunday morning, and the three of us got into "Miss Parklane" and toured Griffith Park. As we drove through this oasis within the city, the beautiful California countryside was sparkling and smogless. We stopped and took pictures of each other overlooking the valley, and of Tim and Tom in the convertible. Tim was tiring very fast, so it was time to go home.

The Fourth of July, 1986, fell on a Sunday, and the way Tim was feeling in the morning we thought that there was not going to be any kind of celebration. By afternoon, he felt a little better, so I made a few sandwiches, took some cookies and fruit and we headed for a nearby park hoping to enjoy this day in the outdoors and be like other people for just a little while.

We found a place away from the other picnickers and spread our blankets. It was late afternoon so the park wasn't crowded. We sat around and ate and enjoyed watching the families as the children played. I used to be so sad that Tim would never have a family of his own; that he would never feel the joy of a child loving him or calling him daddy. That day I was sad because I knew that I would be losing part of my family, my baby, probably before Christmas, maybe much sooner. It started to cool off and we didn't want Tim to catch cold, so we piled in the car and headed for home. He went to bed early while Tom and I enjoyed some of the Lady Liberty festivities on TV.

## Letting Go of Tom

Tim knew he had to let go of Tom, but it was extremely difficult. The day of the Gay Pride Parade and celebration Tom and Jeff went together as Tim was much too ill to go.

It was after they left that he told me how much he loved Tom and how sad he was that they were not going to be together much longer. As he was talking about the parade, he remembered last year's celebration which was shortly after his diagnosis.

He said that as he watched the parade he felt intense anger that this life style that was being celebrated was one of the reasons he was dying. And yet, on reflection he knew he could have done nothing about being homosexual, but he also knew that he could have made better choices concerning his sexual relationships with people.

He told me that he had to allow Tom his freedom, that he couldn't, nor did he want to, keep him a prisoner. Life will have to go on for Tom.

## Tom's Grief

When Tom came home he was crying. He sat down on the sofa and through his tears told me how lonely he was already, and how much he had missed Tim that day. He had also been remembering the previous year's parade, and just the fact that they had been together made things right. Tom was emotionally destroyed. He said, "Bev, we can't let Tim die, we have to find something, we must find something!" I held him and cried with him. "Oh Tom, there is no answer except a miracle and I don't think that is going to happen for Tim." Oh how I wanted to take away the pain and make things better, but I could only cry with him and show him love.

## Sick, And You Visited Me

Friends are so very important at a time like this. One Saturday a group of their friends from San Francisco came to the house to show their love and support. They just wanted to visit and be part of Tim's and Tom's life for the day. When I came home from the grocery store, they were all sitting around the dining room table eating pizza. They had ordered one without cheese for Tim because he could no longer tolerate dairy products. At times like that they didn't need Mom around so I got into the little green Fiesta and headed for one of my refuges, Beverly Center.

I had come to California in July and was preparing to leave in the middle of August. Arrangements had been made through APLA to have an attendant from Progressive Nursing Service come in and spend the days with Tim. He was part of a pilot program to prove how much less it costs for a patient to be cared for in the home rather than having to go to the hospital.

When Tim had to spend time in the hospital I was so thankful that he had such good insurance. I wondered what kind of treatment he would have gotten if he had no insurance, and then I think of those to whom that is a reality. Some of these young men have no partners, no parents, may have been evicted from their homes, have no jobs and are sick in a ward in an AIDS Clinic or even worse, sick in the streets.

*"Then he will say to those on his left hand, 'Depart from me, you cursed, into the eternal fire prepared for the devil and his angels; for I was hungry and you gave me no food, I was thirsty and you gave me no drink, I was a stranger and you did not welcome me,*

*naked and you did not clothe me, sick and in prison
and you did not visit me.' Then they also will answer,
'Lord, when did we see thee hungry or thirsty or a
stranger or naked or sick or in prison?' Then he will
answer them, 'Truly I say to you, as you did it not to
one of the least of these, you did it not to me.' And they
will go away into eternal punishment, but the right-
eous into eternal life."*

Matthew 25: 41-46

**Family Gatherings**

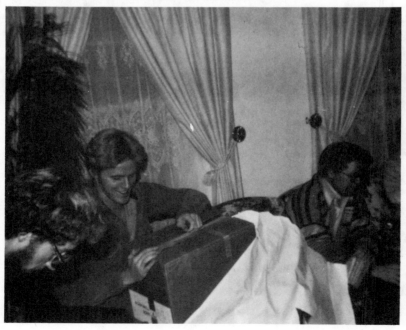

# TWENTY-FOUR

# A Time To Be Together

Tim and I had one more very special day together. One morning he said that he would like to go to a movie. I was very surprised but delighted that he felt up to it, so we scanned the papers and he chose "Back To School." He rested in the morning and was ready to go by mid-afternoon. At the theater he bought a candy bar to eat which concerned me a little bit—but then I thought, let him enjoy what he can at the moment, tomorrow will take care of itself. The movie was very funny and it was so good to hear Tim laugh again.

It was almost time for me to leave California, but there was a mix-up on the paperwork for the nursing service. Dr. Knight had classified Tim as in Stage 3 of the disease, which would call for a registered nurse, while what he really needed was to be classified in Stage 2 so he could qualify for an attendant. Attendants were easier to get than R.N.'s were. My job for the day was to take the papers to Dr. Knight, have him change the classification and get the papers to APLA before they closed. It was close, but I made it. Now the wheels could start moving to get someone to help Tim and Tom.

I was encouraged because the next day a nurse came out to evaluate the situation. There was a minor problem in that they promised that the attendant would be out on Thursday to get acquainted with Tim, the house, and into the swing of things. I was to help with that. No one showed up on Thursday, so I called and found out no one would be there until Monday.

Dave had come out to visit for a couple of days, and since we had flight reservations we had to leave on Friday. Tim would be all right because Tom would be home for the weekend. So Dave and I flew to Las Vegas for a much needed diversion and then home to Lindsborg.

On Monday morning the attendant would be there. None of us should have wasted our time worrying because a very wonderful young man (another Steve) came and did everything that needed to be done and he also became a real friend to Tim and Tom. He had lost his love to this insidious disease, so he knew what the boys were going through.

Tom had planned a trip to Oregon in late August to visit his parents, and he wanted Tim to go with him. I heard about this while I was still in California and thought to myself, "Tim won't be alive at that point."

After Dave and I got home we called Tim almost every day, and we started hearing that he was going to go with Tom. Both of them sounded excited, so Dave and I prayed that the trip would be possible.

## To Be Loved

To prevent the side effects of the chemo while he was in Portland, Tim skipped the treatment the week before he was to leave. Getting there was a nightmare as the whole trip takes seven and one-half hours. First they had to wait at LAX and when their flight was called, Tom wheeled Tim to the plane in a wheel chair. This was the longest stretch of the trip, so it was very fortunate that they had seats in front of the movie screen in a wide body plane. There wasn't anyone around them, so Tim used that whole row as a bed and slept on the way to Portland.

When they reached Portland they had to take a shuttle or small commuter plane to a large island off the coast. This was an ordeal for Tim. From this island they took a boat to the small island where Tom's folks lived. When they arrived, Tim was exhausted and went to bed immediately and stayed there all the next day. Connie and Phil were shocked to see how much Tim had failed since the last time they had seen him.

One of the first things Tom had to do was prepare the bathroom because it was carpeted, and it was now impossible for Tim to control his bowel movements. He found something that was easily cleaned to put over the carpet so Tim didn't have to be concerned about his problem.

The day after they arrived, while Tim was in bed, Connie talked to Tom and told him she knew what both of them were going through. She shared with Tom that her mother, his grandmother, had died at the age of thirty from cancer. She had memories of her mother's pain and helplessness as she spent her days lying on the living room

141

sofa. Tom and his parents had a time of special closeness at this time.

The next day Tim was feeling better. Phil and Connie made it a time of complete rest. Tim could sleep inside or bask in the sun on the beach. Tom was free to do whatever he wanted to do. It was wonderful for me to know that these kind and loving people loved my Tim and were grieving with him in the circumstances of his life. It was a wonderful relaxing time, a time of affirmation of Tim and Tom as a couple and as the wonderful people they were.

The trip home to Los Angeles was not as strenuous because Tom had reserved a beautiful room in one of the best hotels in Portland where he ordered meals from room service so Tim wouldn't have the stress of leaving the room. He had also ordered flowers to make the room more like home. So after a night's rest they caught their flight to LAX and were home again.

## To Die?

Because he missed a couple of chemotherapy sessions, Tim's cancer spread quickly. The small scattered tumors had now fused into larger lesions. His fevers were with him all the time, and his bowel distress was becoming unbearable.

Tim was so distressed that Dr. Knight put him in Sherman Oaks Hospital for transfusions and a re-evaluation. He told Tim that maybe it was time to quit fighting and die with dignity. He would supply him with pain medication intravenously and Tim could regulate it himself. He more or less gave Tim permission to leave when things got too bad.

Dr. Rarick called me in Lindsborg. He told me that if Tim would fight and take the chemo he might have another six months. I asked if the quality of his life would improve and he told me no, but he didn't want Tim to give up. He was trying everything he knew to help.

Dr. Rarick had decided that the combination of two chemicals would work as well as the three and that there would be minimal side effects.

Dave and I made many calls to the hospital. Tim told us that because Dr. Knight and Dr. Rarick couldn't positively diagnose his bowel problem, but since they believed it was the cancer, he would continue with the chemo. He had a heplock in place and was getting dilaudid, a pain medication. He was going home and a nurse and Tom would administer his medication until I got there. I made reservations for Friday, September 12, 1986.

"God, is this the last time I will be called upon to go and help with Tim's life? Will this time bring the greater good: Tim's transition from this life to the next? I don't know what to hope for or how to pray."

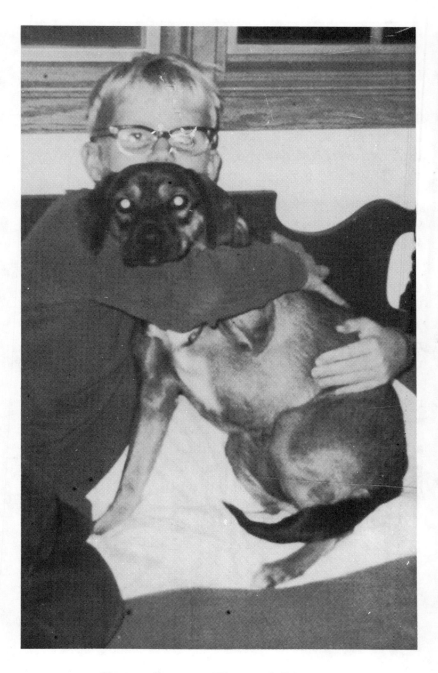

**Puppy Love — Tim and Ginger**

# TWENTY-FIVE

## The Last Time

### September 12, 1986

September 12th arrived and Dave took me to the air-port. We didn't know what to say to each other except "I love you." There was nothing extraordinary about my plane ride. I had time to think. I wondered how many more wonderful people had to die before a cure for this terrible plague is found. In anger and frustration I wept before God. "Where are you for this boy who has already suffered so much in his young life? Take away his anxiety, give him peace and the assurance of your presence. Heal him or kill him! Give his life some quality or take him home to be with you."

Tom had feelings of guilt. In a phone conversation he expressed that he hadn't done enough to encourage Tim to fight, that after the trip to Portland he hadn't come up with anything else that would have made Tim want to go on. I assured Tom that he had nothing to feel guilty about, that he was the best partner anyone could have asked for.

After landing at LAX, I picked up my luggage and got on the Super Shuttle once more. Once on our way, the lady in front of me started a conversation. It seems she was the head of the state nurses' association and had come to Los Angeles to address nurses at a seminar on AIDS. We had a discussion about Tim's situation and I found her very sympathetic. When she left the shuttle she gave me her card and said that if there was anything she could do, to call her.

My feelings were that there was nothing anyone could do now, that it was just a waiting game for the inevitable end.

As I entered the house Tim was on the sofa and Tommy, home from work, was about to give him an injection for the pain. I got down on my knees and watched closely as Tom explained it to me in detail, because I would be the one doing it most of the time from now on.

I was to take out two new needles (syringes), the medication and the flush, also the alcohol swabs. First I must wipe the top of the medication and flush bottles with alcohol swabs, then wipe the surface of the heparin lock with another swab. The procedure was as follows: take one syringe out of its container, plunge it into the medication bottle, measure the dilaudid carefully, take it out and push it slightly so there were no air bubbles. The center of the heparin lock is soft and spongy so the needle goes in there easily. Slowly I would squeeze the drug into Tim's body. The effect was almost instantaneous. Then I would take the other syringe, fill it with flush, get rid of any bubbles and flush the heparin lock. This kept it from

146

getting clogged.

By this time the bowel blockage was so great that he had to stand to have any relief. The effort was so enormous and the pain so extreme that Tim waited to go to the bathroom until just before he was to get a dilaudid injection. He felt so bad about the messes in the bathroom, but I told him that it was no fault of his as there was nothing he could do about it. I took old towels and put around the commode which I could rinse out and put in the washer. We used bleach and more bleach in the house. Through all of this the only precaution we had to take was to wear hospital gloves which were then thrown away.

We decided to have the attendant continue coming, because if I would have to leave for any reason it might have been difficult to get the program in motion again. The attendant who had been coming up to now was going back to school and would no longer be available. This was too bad because he was kind and efficient, and Tim liked and trusted him.

There was no way to know who the next attendant would be. Monday morning, a young woman showed up and said she reporting for work. Her name was Letitia and she had been a registered nurse in Mexico. She was going to school so she would be able to be licensed as an R.N. in this country.

All of the attendants seemed to have a different understanding of their duties. While Steve would cook, clean up the whole house and do all laundry and dishes, Letitia said it was her job to do only Tim's wash and dishes (she wouldn't use the dishwasher) and keep only the immediate area around where Tim ate and slept clean. She would also cook for him and clean the bathroom. The first time she did laundry, she got some of Tom's clothes in with Tim's. She used so much bleach that she ruined about a hundred dollars worth of clothes. Tom was so angry that he told me not to allow her to wash anything. So after that, I did the laundry.

I know it was difficult for the attendants to have me around all the time and I was somewhat uncomfortable too. I often wondered what my role really was, but after listening to the boys, I believed that it was necessary for me to be there.

Fixing breakfast was my job because Tim wanted to eat before the attendant (whoever it was) got there. Sometimes, after he showered and shaved, we would go for a short walk to the end of the block and back. Occasionally he would get carried away and want to walk around the block, but we soon learned that it wasn't very wise because he would barely make it back. After the walk he would try to sleep for awhile and then I would just keep him company, sometimes talking, reading to him or simply watching TV.

The attendants would leave at 4:00 P.M., and then I would fix the evening meal and do dishes before bedtime. Most of the time the boys and I would watch a little television and they would retire early. Tom had to be up between 4:30 and 5:00 A.M. so he couldn't stay awake past 8:00 P.M. Their favorite programs were Card Sharks and Mr. Ed. Mr. Ed could usually get a laugh, even from Tim.

Tim's diet was very limited, no sugar, no dairy foods, no preservatives, nothing that was difficult to digest and not much red meat. With all these restrictions, Tim was also very fussy. One day I had a food breakdown; I couldn't think of anything to prepare. Tommy ordered vegetarian pizza with no cheese to be sent in. Bless him. It was at this point that Tim started taking a digestive enzyme and Milk of Magnesia to help aid the digestive system and to keep his body waste moving.

Tim had a Wednesday afternoon appointment with Dr. Knight. It was raining as we got into the car, and I knew Tim was concerned—rush hour traffic in the rain. After driving a few blocks, he told me to pull over, find a telephone and cancel the appointment. I knew the situation was bad but didn't know how bad until that evening when the newscaster reported how many accidents there had been on Hollywood Freeway. I thought, "That could have been us. It would have been extremely bad to have been in an accident or even caught in traffic with Tim so ill." He was very relieved that we had aborted the trip.

The appointment was rescheduled for Thursday morning. Dr. Knight examined Tim and found that he needed another blood transfusion. He asked him if he wanted to go through with it as it wouldn't really do any good except to make him feel better. Tim said that he wanted the transfusion, so the nurse came in and took blood for cross-matching.

Dr. Knight wanted me to come in and look at the large herpetic sore on Tim's coxyx because he wanted it cleaned and bandaged every day. A special bandage had to be used, so he gave us a supply of them. Then when we ordered our regular supplies (syringe, dilaudid, flush, alcohol swabs) we ordered the breathing bandages also.

Tim had barely made it home from the doctor's office

that day, and after he crawled into bed he got a call from the nurse telling us we had to go back to Sherman Oaks for them take more blood. We left a message for Dr. Knight, and when he returned our call he assured us that it wasn't necessary. Thinking everything had been taken care of, we didn't concern ourselves with it anymore.

On Friday morning Letitia arrived late and Tim was not at all well. Someone from the lab at Sherman Oaks called again and said that Tim had to come in to have some more blood drawn. We told them to check with Dr. Knight because he said that it wasn't necessary.

I had just given Tim a shot of dilaudid and having been assured that we wouldn't have to go to the hospital again, I decided to go to Beverly Center for two hours. As I was to find out later, this was a bad time to leave, because while I was gone, the hospital called again, Dr. Knight's nurse, Jeannine called, Progressive Nursing (they provided the attendants) called, and Lifeline (the organization which delivered our supplies) called.

Jeannine told Tim he had to go to the hospital again. Progressive Nursing wanted to check on giving chemo at home and Lifeline was inquiring about what supplies we would be needing for the next week.

Meanwhile, I had a strange feeling that there may have been trouble at home, so I called from the shopping center. Tim was in tears because he couldn't cope with the situation. I returned home and called everyone back to get things straightened out. I settled everything with Jeannine, ordered our supplies, and Progressive Nursing sent out a nurse, Joe, to take enough blood for cross-matching and to discuss chemotherapy at home.

# TWENTY-SIX

## As Life Goes On

### September 27, 1986

Saturday, September 27, 1986, was to be transfusion day. I rose early and called the hospital to make sure everything was ready. It seemed that they had the blood; however, Dr. Knight hadn't left an order. So I called him (woke him up) and he called the hospital to make the arrangements.

Tom drove Tim to the hospital and stayed while I did the grocery shopping and some house cleaning. In the middle of the afternoon I went to the hospital to relieve Tom. Tim was very agitated and under constant stress. He questioned whether or not the blood was dripping properly. He felt the nurses were incompetent and was disappointed with the food because there was nothing served that he could eat. Because of the transfusion he had to urinate often and his bowel was giving him problems, so he had to get in and out of bed often, which was an extreme hassle. Finally it was done.

On Sunday, Tim wasn't feeling as well as he usually does after a transfusion, but Tom was determined to get him out of the house for awhile. So after the household chores were finished Tim, Tom, and Jeff went for a ride in "Miss Parklane." Just this short outing took its toll on Tim, and when they came back he went to bed immediately.

Tom and Jeff went out for awhile. The house was quiet, and it was a good time for me to call Pam and catch up on all the family news. She reported that Colleen was in a dance class and Sean was taking instruction in Kung Fu. Colleen got on the phone and asked, "Grandma, will Uncle Tim be able to come and see me the next time you come?" With tears in my eyes I had to tell her that Uncle Tim was very sick and probably would never see her again. Many people had been praying for Tim, and Sean and Colleen were two of the best pray-ers in the world. They believed that when they asked God for Uncle Tim to be healed, he would be, and that was that. How does one argue with that kind of faith?

## Who Will the Next One Be?

Another Monday morning and apprehension was setting in. Who would we get as an attendant today? (Letitia had been put in charge of someone who was alone and needed more extensive nursing care.) All of us prayed that we would get someone kind and compatible. The doorbell rang and a young woman named Jessica was at the door.

She seemed very nice and was willing to do everything. Tim got up in a good mood and started to shower. I had fixed him a good breakfast, which he had almost finished by the time Jessica arrived. He was settled in in front of the television when I left for a long walk. I didn't have my watch, so I was extremely conscious of the time. After a time I walked by a restaurant that had a clock which could be seen from the door and realized that I had only fifteen minutes until I was due to give Tim a pain injection. By the time I got home, Tim was giving himself the injection with his left hand into the heplock on his right wrist. He wanted to prove to himself that he could do it if he had to. This made me very nervous—and after this it was always on my mind—I did get a watch.

Tom always went to bed shortly after supper. He and I were starting a diet, which was a big laugh, because neither of us had any willpower in that area. When we were under stress, we would poke our heads into the refrigerator and say, "What's to eat?" Cooking nourishing and fattening foods for Tim had put weight on Tom and me. I had put on about 20 pounds, and Tom at 5' 10" was hitting 200 pounds—and Tim got thinner and thinner.

By this time Tim had lost all of his self-consciousness, and he would come out of the bathroom without his shorts on. It didn't matter because now I was bandaging the sore on his coxyx every day, and he was to allow the air to circulate as much as possible.

Tuesday was Jessica's second day, and she came late. When she finally arrived she was coughing and said she had chills. I couldn't believe it; why had she come at all? I sent her home because Tim didn't need her infection. When she got home she called her service and told them that she really wasn't sick, but that I had sent her home because I thought she was sick.

We got through that day without an attendant. It was

almost a blessing to have the house to ourselves.

## Planning the Service

Tim and I had the opportunity to discuss death and dying. What did he want for a memorial service? We agreed that it shouldn't be a "funeral," but a celebration of his life. Soon it would be time for his transition—from this life to the next. What did he want the service to say about him?

We discussed the music and we decided on **"It Is Well With My Soul,"** because of our faith that through all of this we could both feel peace, knowing that he would be in God's presence. Bill Gaither's **"It Is Finished"** would be a part of the service. We knew that because of Christ's death on the cross, Tim's suffering would indeed be finished.

Tim had been involved in prayer and meditation, and as he has been so close to death he had experienced the white light vision. Now he would soon be with the source of that light.

As we talked about music, we recalled how important music has been in his life. When he was a baby I would sing as I rocked him to sleep, and when he was old enough he learned to sing the nursery rhymes and the children's choruses from Sunday School.

While he was going through his eye surgeries, his favorite singer was Mahalia Jackson and his favorite song was **"Holy, Holy, Holy."** He used to sit for hours and look at her picture on the record jacket while he listened to her music. One day when going to the eye doctor, we got on an elevator which was being run by a large black lady. Tim got this awe-struck look on his face and blurted out, **"Holy, Holy, Holy."** Needless to say I had to explain what he meant, and we all had a good laugh about it.

Yes, Tim remembered piano practices and recitals, cello practice and the orchestra as well as the vocal groups he had been part of. These indeed had provided him pleasure, but it could never compensate for not being "one of the boys."

The next attendant we got was a young man named Mike. He was very hyperactive, yet extremely efficient. When he finished his work, I would tell him, "For heaven's sake, sit down and watch your soaps." He was also planning to become an R.N. and was going to start school shortly.

Although Mike was very talkative, he was easy to have around, and both Tim and I were very comfortable with him.

## Final Arrangements

One of the most difficult things for me to do was to go to the mortuary while Tim was still alive and make final arrangements for services. Tom could not do this because a relative had to sign the papers. The hospital had given Tom a list of mortuaries whose people had no hesitations about taking the body of an AIDS victim. When the epidemic began this was a major problem, and many were turned away. I was very thankful that attitudes had changed.

As I drove to Abbott and Hast Mortuary on Venice

Boulevard I thought, this isn't right, I should be making arrangements for my mother, or Tim should be making arrangements for me, not a mother for her son.

A young gentlemen whose name was Chester greeted me and immediately put me at ease. The people who own and manage this mortuary are very sympathetic to the family and partners of AIDS victims. Chester asked me about Tim and Tom and what our families were like. Then he told me some very personal things about himself. He had lost his partner and his father within a few months of each other, and he had handled both funerals. He was a very strong and kind man.

After this time of sharing, I told him what Tim and I wanted for a service, promised him the tapes with the music at the appropriate time, signed the papers and went home. "Thank you, Chester."

## For Sale

The house had been up for sale for some time, and one day the landlord told us that there were people interested in buying it, and by law it had to be fumigated before the deal could be closed. Earlier in the summer a middle-aged couple had come through the house. Tim was on the sofa and just by his appearance, they had to know that he was very ill. This couple seemed to be very kind and compassionate, and Tim, Tom and I liked them immediately; however, we didn't want to move, so we hoped that they wouldn't want the house.

Now it appeared that they were the interested party because no one else had come through. A great deal of work had to be done on the house, so plumbers, carpenters, electricians and inspectors all started coming through. It proved to be a very noisy, unsettling time, putting stress on every aspect of our lives together. For the fumigation process, we would have to move out for one night and stay away until the next afternoon.

Two days before the fumigation we had a change in attendants again. Mike went back to working full time for a former patient of his, who was dying, and Stuart arrived at our house. All of the changes in attendants were very stressful for Tim and me. Tim cried when this new person showed up because he had to adjust all over again. When a person is very ill and has so many intimately personal problems it can be very humiliating to trust oneself into the care of a new person every week, even though it is out of the patient's control. However, Stuart fit in very well; he was extremely kind and considerate.

The day before the fumigation process, Stuart, Tom and I wrapped everything that could be harmed by the chemicals; we put all perishables that didn't need refrigeration in "Miss Parklane" and pulled her into the garage. Items that needed refrigeration we packed in the other cars and took then over to Everett's and John's house.

These two young men were so kind as they let us stay with them while the fumigation took place. They had a large, very spacious apartment where Tim and Tom had the extra bedroom with a half bath and I slept in the living room. They had two cats, Freeway and Charlie, who were extremely entertaining as the younger teased the older to distraction, and the situation would end up in a lively chase and a friendly fight. Tim enjoyed having the animals around; they were good therapy.

Everett was out of town, so John acted as host. After supper, Tim and Tom went to bed, and John and I stayed up and had a wonderful time of sharing. He said that as he grew up he always tried to stay out of the way; he didn't make waves and he didn't call attention to himself. He knew he was different but again really didn't know what to do about the difference. His father was very ill while John was in high school and died shortly after John's graduation. He and Everett had been together for many years and yet he told me, "Bev, if I had a choice I would have a wife, three kids and live in the suburbs; however, that is not possible for me, so I live my life the best way I can within the parameters I am given."

The next day Tom stopped on the way home from work to open up the house and let it air out. There was to be a lot of work ahead of us because we wanted to wash everything that the poisonous chemicals had come in contact with. That evening Tom and I washed cupboards and cleaned the refrigerator so that food could be put away again.

Stuart came back the next morning and helped clean shelves and the stove and wash dishes, for which I shall be eternally grateful. It was just another hurdle to cross.

The sale of the house was completed, and one morning the new landlord came by to talk to me. He had surmised what Tim's problem was and wanted to assure all of us that Tim and Tom would not be evicted. He owned a number of rental units and had encountered this situation before. He knew it would be too much for Tom and Tim to have to leave their home and search for a new one during Tim's dying process. He was buying the building so that his daughter and her children could move into the part of the house we were in at the time—however, he said his daughter could wait. My tears came; I cried, "Thank you, Sir!" "Thank you, God."

## With Love from Mike, Pam and Dad

At different times during Tim's last few weeks at home, Dave, Pam and Mike had come out to California to visit him.

During Mike's visit, Tim really pushed himself so that he would appear healthier than he really was. The brothers had a wonderful time together, a terrific final communication. I made lunch and by the time everyone had finished, it was apparent that Tim couldn't take anymore. Tim excused himself and went to bed, and I took Mike for a tour of Hollywood. After our ride, we visited Beverly Center and the grocery store. Mike decided that if he would have to put up with all the traffic and stress, he would be sick too. The relative peace and quiet of Garden City, Kansas, looked pretty good at that time.

All of us spent the evening together, first dinner and then a short time of fellowship until bedtime. Mike did get sick that night and spent part of the time worshipping on his knees in front of the porcelain shrine. By the middle of the next morning he was on his way to the airport. "Thank you for coming, Mike."

Pam's visit was like a refreshing breeze in this household of sickness and impending death. She loved Tim fiercely and did everything to cheer him up and to keep everything on a positive note. Pam could talk to Tim about anything. They remembered the past, discussed the present, and could deal with the future. Tim was so happy to have her there.

One morning, Jeff invited all of us to his house for brunch. All of the food was wonderful, and Jeff was indeed the "hostess with the mostest." After brunch all of the goodbyes were said (very special between Tim and Pam), and Tom took Tim home while I drove Pam to the airport. "Goodbye Pam, Thank you for a wonderful time of Love."

Dave came out to spend a few days with his son. The most memorable time for both Dave and Tim was the day they walked together through Forest Lawn Cemetery. As they read the names and messages on the various memorial stones, they could talk easily about what they meant to each other, about death, and about their faith in God's promise for eternity. This was the last time for father and son to be alone together. "Thank you, Dave for loving and caring."

## Hospital

A few weeks had passed since Tim's last transfusion and he was in need of another. There always seemed to be a problem typing Tim's blood for cross-matching, which caused more stress. Tim was to get three pints this time. The lab at Sherman Oaks Hospital called and told us that the blood was ready. When we arrived they had only two pints but continued to search for a third while the first two were being transfused.

Fortunately another pint was located. This procedure took all day, and many things took place that made Tim and me question whether or not the nurses knew what they were doing. At first they had to find a good vein, and there was discussion as to how to do this the best way— hot towels or no hot towels seemed to be the question. There is a computerized system for administering the blood via an intravenous pump, and not all the nurses seemed to know how it worked. Finally the head nurse came in and got it going. It was also time for a new heplock to be put in. The old one would be left in for pain medication while he was being transfused and taken out before we left the hospital.

After being in bed all day, Tim was feeling tired and extremely agitated. To finish the day off with a bang, the pump was not adjusted correctly and when the hook-up was released, blood spurted all over.

As we left the hospital, feeling very angry, little did we know that Tim would be back in a week, this time to stay, and we would discover that these same nurses were really very competent and caring angels of mercy.

Later in the week Tim was to have another chemotherapy session. It was to be done at home by a nurse from the Progressive Nursing Service. The chemicals were delivered early that day and the nurse, a very capable and efficient young man, joked with Tim as the treatment took place.

Since the change in the chemical mix, there were few side effects. Yet it was very destructive to the blood count, so it could almost neutralize the positive effects of the transfusion. The chemo did seem to aggravate the bowel problem and caused Tim extreme discomfort the next day.

## Have a Wonderful Time, Tom

Tom had known for a long time that he would have to go to Portland for his brother's wedding as he was to serve as best man. He hesitated about going because he didn't know if Tim would still be alive when he got back.

I promised to take good care of Tim, and that I would notify him if anything out of the ordinary happened. Tim and Tom had some very private moments together as they said goodbye to each other, "just in case."

Tom needed to get away and this was a wonderful opportunity. He would be with his family and friends, and perhaps he would be able to forget for just a little while. None of us knew it was to be this weekend that Tim was supposed to die.

# TWENTY-SEVEN

## Mom, Is It Time To Die?

### Nurses, Bells and Bears

Tim didn't die that Saturday night, October 25th, nor did he die on Sunday. Tom was back from Portland and spent the first few nights at the hospital. Late one night I got a call from the hospital; one of the nurses advised me to come back. Tim's fever was up, and his heart (he ordinarily had an irregular heart beat) was beating so hard and so rapidly that it was possible that he could die anytime.

I hurried back to the hospital, got in the elevator, and pushed the button for the third floor. Tommy was extremely concerned and yet peaceful. As I think about it now, I know he was so exhausted that he could barely function. Tom went to lie down on the rollaway, and I sat in the chair next to Tim and held his hand.

I sat there and told him how much we loved him and would miss him, but if the pain and anguish were too great, he could leave if he wanted to. In the middle of all this he opened his eyes, looked at me, and said, "Mom, I think they are making too big a deal of this, I don't think I am that sick." I put my hand on his forehead and said, "If you really believe that, then you probably aren't ready to go yet." By Tuesday, he was up and walking around the halls with me pulling his intravenous pump, trying my best to keep up with him. Dr. Knight came up, took one look and had to find a place to sit down as he exclaimed, "I don't believe what I am seeing."

The diet that was ordered for Tim was first a liquid diet and, later in the week, a bland diet. Meal times were not very exciting. He made a valiant effort to eat and drink, trying to figure out how much was going in and how much was coming out. The bowel problem just kept getting worse, but we knew that the obstruction was not total.

Whenever Tim had to use the bathroom, we would unplug the intravenous pumps delivering the antibiotic and the morphine and wheel them into the bathroom with him. In the beginning this worked very well as his pain was not as intense as it had been at home because of the steady infusion of the morphine.

The morphine was, however, a two-edged sword, because the more he took, the more it slowed the natural action of the bowel. Some days he would turn down the morphine just to see if his body functioned better. It didn't seem to make much difference, except to make him uncomfortable, so he would turn it up again at night so he could sleep.

Those wonderful computerized machines, what inventions. If the level of the medication, or in case of a transfusion, the level of the blood got low, bells would start ringing. This also occurred if there was any problem with the delivery of medication or blood, so it was almost foolproof. No one could ignore those bells for any prolonged period of time, so the patient knew he would be getting someone's attention.

Within the first week, Tim was strong enough to get in and out of the bathtub with help. Twice that week he had a tub bath, with sponge baths the rest of the time.

## Tom's Love

Tim was very fastidious about his person, so he also wanted his hair washed. Tommy pulled a chair into the little bathroom, put a towel on it, found some carpet scraps to put under Tim's feet and opened "Tom's Sherman Oaks Beauty Shoppe" for only one person, his beloved Tim. As Tom washed Tim's hair, it seemed to make Tim feel much better. Again, I have seen love.

## Of Life and Death

Veins were not made for the kind of abuse given when someone is this ill. Dr. Knight thought that it was time for a subclavian catheter to be put into Tim's chest so that his medication could be infused directly via the catheter. There would be no more hunting for veins to put the heplock into. It was such a simple operation, yet I wondered, if this type of surgery could be done and the patient heals, why couldn't they go in and take a look at the obstruction. So I asked about it. Dr. Knight told me that the exploratory surgery would be much more extensive and that in Tim's weakened condition he probably couldn't survive it. Also, it would pose a much more serious threat of infection and more misery for something that couldn't be cured.

Later I reflected on this and wondered if Tim had had surgery at a very early stage if it would have helped? Then I considered the fact that the cancer would have killed him some other way—I guess it really wouldn't have made any difference.

Tim still believed there might be a chance. Dr. Olson, an oncologist, was looking in on Tim on Dr. Knight's days off. One day Tim asked if chemo might help him. Dr. Olson told him that considering his weakened condition, chemotherapy would probably make things worse by opening his lesions and might increase his pain to a point where morphine might not be enough to keep him comfortable. He also said that if AIDS could be cured he would give chemo a try; however, death was still the ever-present reality and the only outcome, so why suffer unnecessarily?

The hospital staff was wonderful. Our social worker told me, "If you have to have AIDS, Sherman Oaks Hospital is the place to have it." Each patient was treated with dignity and care. If a personality conflict occurred between patient and nurse, the two would not be put together again except in an extreme emergency.

One evening the regular nurse called in ill, so a replacement was located from an agency. He appeared to be a very efficient young man, so Tom and I went home believing that Tim would be well cared for. Later as Tim was standing by his bed he developed heart palpitations and fell to the floor. Try as he may, he could not control his bodily functions, so he cried out for help.

The nurse, the new kid on the block, came in and after seeing what was happening called out for the other nurses to come because he couldn't handle the situation. Everyone came running and, to Tim's shame and humiliation, viewed him lying on the floor in his own wastes.

After he was cleaned up and back in bed, he called me crying and said something terrible had happened that evening and he didn't ever want that nurse in his room again. He never did tell me exactly what had happened. It was the other nurses on duty who told me the story and that the situation should have been handled differently, for although it was just one of those things that happen on that floor, it was totally dehumanizing to Tim. That particular nurse was not put in charge of the critically ill again.

The nurses who constantly care for these young men have to have a sense of humor and also a strong faith of some kind to be able to continue within the realm of reason and sanity. So many young men are dying here believing they are unforgiven by man and God because of their lifestyle. Donna told me of a patient, we'll call him Eric, who came from a Pentecostal background. The two of them had shared their faith and discovered that they believed in many of the same things. One day his pain was becoming unbearable and he called to her to come in and pray. Donna laid hands on Eric and prayed in her special gift of tongues. A peace descended upon the room, and Eric was released from the racking pain and the unthinkable fear that had gripped his body a short time before.

There was a remission long enough to start the regular drip, drip of the pain medication that would, through the efforts of man, numb his brain, making him oblivious to the messages of his body.

## Thoughts of any of the critical AIDS patients...

"This truly is a dying place ... the crying place. Is it time to choose how to die? What is a dignified death?

"If I refuse the precious liquid calories and starve to death, is that the right thing to do? Shall I say, no oxygen or respirator, and suffocate or choke to death, is that the best way? Perhaps I should refuse the medications and the transfusions thereby depriving my body of its life blood. I will give up all of these things and let the bacteria, the viruses, the parasites and whatever else there is, gnaw away at me until I am no more. Turn up the morphine— turn out the world—there are too many choices, yet there are none."

Many people came to visit Tim, just to let him know that they cared and that their thoughts and prayers were with him. Almost everyone brought something ... a humorous card, a balloon bouquet, flowers or a Teddy bear. They didn't just look in and say hello, but stayed and talked, making him part of their lives, at least for a little while. He knew that these were truly good friends.

Johnny and Jack brought a bear that had a musical system of bells which was supposed to be activated by the clapping of hands. Well, it seemed that any sharp noise turned the bear's bells on and it would play its repertoire of nursery rhymes. At first this was very confusing for the nurses, for when they heard the bells they thought it meant that something was amiss that set off the computerized pump in the patient's room. After a short adjustment period they would listen for a few minutes before coming into Tim's room. If they heard **"Twinkle, Twinkle Little Star,"** or **"Jack and Jill"** (among others), they knew it was Belle the Bear and that they were not being summoned.

There got to be such a collection of cards, balloons, stuffed animals and flowers, that the cleaning lady had to rearrange things just to get to the surface of the furniture. It had to be somewhat frustrating because that is the way it was in most of the rooms on the AIDS floor. Yet they didn't complain. I believe that everyone that worked on that floor had been selected for their kindness, compassion, and sense of humor.

Because Tim was receiving so many visitors, he needed something to wear that would make him feel presentable. Hospital gowns are not made to cover the average person adequately and are absolutely indecent on someone who is over six feet tall. As Tim lay in his bed attempting to keep himself covered, Tom and I would run to the storage closet and look through the gowns trying to find the longest one. Finally I decided to do something about it.

There was one small shop at Beverly Center which always had a rack of items for $10. It was there I found three, long, oversize T-shirts, one pink, one pale green and one yellow. It was a simple matter to cut them up the back, hem the raw edge and sew on bias tape to be used as ties in the back.

Tim was much more comfortable in these home-made

T-shirt gowns than the hospital "uniforms," because they were soft and warm. They were long enough so that some of his modesty could be preserved. The pastel colors also softened the pallor of sickness and death that was reflected in his face.

## Visit from Alexis

Shortly after Halloween, Rick, a dear friend, came up to see Tim. Rick is a very masculine young man with full mustache and a very hairy body. This particular night he looked different, in fact quite different. He came into the room and started talking to Tim and Tom. I stared at him, not able to figure out what was different about him. After all, it had been a long time since I had seen him. He was telling about the Halloween party he had attended dressed as Alexis from Dynasty. (Oh yes, he had shaved off every hair that was visible.)

As he described the party, we could imagine what a vision of loveliness he must have been. Tim was laughing and said that he sure would like to have seen Rick as Alexis.

The next day Rick called to tell me that he would cook dinner for all of us, bring it up to the hospital room and serve us. None of us ate anything after lunch that day, anticipating the dinner Rick promised. He knew what Tim could tolerate, so we all looked forward to a fine meal. Late in the afternoon the elevator opened and we heard the theme from Dynasty begin. Rick walked in looking more like Alexis than Alexis. He had a high fashioned white hat, beautifully-coiffured wig, a well-proportioned, albeit contrived figure, complete with a gorgeous white dress, gloves, spike-heeled shoes and a fur casually thrown over his shoulders. Needless to say, he was the center of attention. The staff took turns coming in just to look. The female nurses and I said, "We should look so good."

Rick had made the ultimate sacrifice again as he shaved everything that showed. He was even taped up to show cleavage. It seems that when he got out of his car, a security guard asked him if he was busy later that evening. In his low masculine voice he said, "Why no, honey." The guard almost passed out and made himself very scarce. At least Rick didn't see him again.

After his initial appearance, Rick, Tom and I went down to his car to get the dinner fixings. Rick wanted to create an ambiance or mood different from the usual hospital atmosphere. He brought out his good china and crystal, candles and holders and proceeded to set up a lovely buffet on the extra moveable table in the room.

He had prepared a wonderful chicken dish which he served with french bread. It was a wonderful welcome meal which we washed down with the excellent wine he supplied.

After stuffing ourselves and enjoying each other's company, Rick visited every room on the AIDS ward as Alexis from Dynasty. A good time was had by all.

Through the first week in November, Tim was moving around fairly well. He could get in and out of bed and stand, so he was able to use the urinal and walk to the bathroom and back. This was a difficult procedure because he was hooked up to various numbers of intravenous pumps which were mounted on two poles and moved around on casters. Tim always needed help to get the machines unplugged and rolled with him wherever he went. There was so much tubing involved that is was difficult to keep track of which tube was feeding him what. Even the nurses had to carefully follow each tube back to the machine when it was time to administer medication via the tube or when it was time to change the tubing.

The subclavian catheter made life easier for Tim because it eliminated the need for the heplock in the arms, so there were no more pokings and stickings to find a vein.

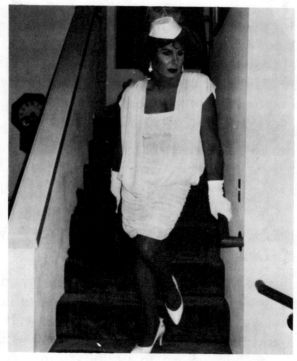

**Rick as "Alexis"**

# TWENTY-EIGHT

# Happy Birthday Dear Tim
# Happy Birthday To You

## Tim is 27

It was soon to be Tim's birthday, his 27th. Was it his goal to live until then? Everyone was amazed that he was still alive. November 11th came, and there was another avalanche of cards wishing Tim the best. Most of them were chosen with love and concern hoping to give Tim something to smile about or, yes, even laugh about for a few minutes.

Colleen and Sean colored pictures for their Uncle Tim, which were taped to the front of the refrigerator door in Tim's room. We had many family pictures scattered around to remind Tim that he was loved. A small package and letter from Mike arrived which Tim opened with eagerness. The package contained a small plaque on which was written a poem about the importance of family.

As Tim read the letter tears rolled down his checks. I read it and cried and had to thank God for Mike's tender heart and for sharing his love and sorrow with his brother.

Some weeks before, when Tim was still at home, he had received a letter from Tom's brother. It too was uplifting and affirming for Tim, as he bravely fought for his life. (Both of these letters were used at the memorial service; therefore, they are recorded in a later chapter.)

Tom arrived at the hospital a little later than usual because he was searching for some red gladiolas, which was their special flower. When he came, he had the flowers, a colorful birthday tablecloth which we taped to the wall, a bottle of champagne, a tiny Teddy bear, many balloons, and a very special card. Tom knew that Tim couldn't have real cake, so he found an inflatable cake complete with candles which he presented to Tim and we sang **"Happy Birthday."**

I had made cupcakes the night before and although Tim couldn't eat them, the doctors, nurses and visitors had a chance to enjoy them. Jeff and Everett came to help us celebrate Tim's 27th birthday, the birthday we didn't think he would live to see, in fact, that I had prayed that he wouldn't. That evening we offered toasts to Tim's life and what he had meant to each of us. Tim couldn't partake of the champagne, but he joined us in the love and fellowship of that evening. The decorations stayed but eventually started to fade just as Tim was fading.

## Dramas of Courage

In all the rooms on 3 West, similar dramas were being played out. When Tim was admitted, Steve Kant's partner was in the next room. Max had a virus called Cytome-galovirus (CMV), which the doctors were fighting with experimental drugs. It is a common virus found in the general population which causes flu-like symptoms and is very short-lived. In the AIDS patient, however, it local-izes in one part of the body and does not go away. If it attacks the eyes it causes blindness; in Max it invaded his intestinal track, making him unable to retain or utilize his food.

I would go in and talk with him. We talked about family. Max didn't have much contact with anyone except an aunt, his Godmother, who loved and appreciated him for who he was—nothing else mattered to her. He was so very ill that I kept my visits short, not wanting to overtire him.

Concerning his illness, he said, "Bev, if anyone had ever told me that I would cling to this life through every-thing I have experienced, I would have said they were crazy. But, here I am, hanging on no matter what, always thinking maybe this is the day that something will be found that will save me. I am always setting a new goal for myself, a new time frame to live through. There is a cabin in the mountains that holds a lot of memories for me. Steve and I have spent many happy holidays there. Maybe if I live to Thanksgiving, I can make one last trip to our cabin."

Max did get better, in fact well enough to go home, but he died two months after Tim. The disease starved him to death.

## Weeping for Our Children

On the other side of Tim was a man with pneumocystis pneumonia. He was in his mid-forties. We'll call him Adam. All day and every night we would hear him cough until he would end up in a fit of choking. We wondered how long he could he possibly last? The coughing made Tim so nervous that we considered asking the nurses if Adam could be moved; however, then we realized that those three rooms held the patients considered most critical, Tim, Max and Adam, who required the most care, so Adam had to stay.

Adam's parents were with him. His father was in control of his emotions, but his mother, Sarah, was absolutely devastated. She cried and cried, fingering her rosary and asking God to help her son. As I appeared to be handling my situation quite well, the nurses asked me if I would talk to Sarah.

I introduced myself and after I told Tim where I would be. Sarah and I went to a conference room that was more private than the hall. Sarah's first question to me was, "Why is God punishing us and our sons, why did they have to get this terrible and shameful disease, and why do they have to die?"

I told her that, in my opinion, it had nothing to do with punishment, that this was a human condition, that we just happened to get caught at a time when there was no cure for this specific disease, and that through the years many people had been caught in the same situation with other diseases.

She felt some guilt because of Adam's lifestyle and

thought that if she hadn't allowed him to go to California things might have been different. I said, "Sarah, Adam is who he is, where he lived would have made no difference even if you had the influence to keep him at home." It is such a dilemma even for parents to understand that their homosexual children have no choice in their sexual preferences. We always seem to believe that somehow it was our fault and that we could have done something to fix it.

Going out to coffee, Sarah and I continued to talk and she seemed to feel better; at least she appeared to be more peaceful. She said her rosary and prayed for a peaceful death for Adam.

That is what I desired for Tim. All of these fine young men will die. It is indeed a time of great sorrow.

*"Thus says the Lord: A voice is heard in Ramah, lamentation and bitter weeping. Rachel is weeping for her children; she refuses to be comforted for her children, because they are not."*

Jeremiah 31:15

Day after day, Sarah and her husband were there and Adam's friends were in and out. One night it seemed that death was upon him, but suddenly the pneumocystis seemed to loosen its grip, and Adam checked himself out of the hospital to live out his life at home.

## When There is Nothing Left, Remember

Roger and Fred were another devoted couple. Roger and I first met each other on the elevator and greeted each other as we walked the halls while Tim and Fred were sleeping. Finally we started talking and became friends. It was very difficult for Roger because there was no communication with his loved one because Fred was on a respirator. Toxoplasmosis was the diagnosis, and at this point he couldn't breathe on his own.

Roger invited me out for dinner one evening, so we made a quick trip to Hamburger Hamlet. He was an extraordinary young man with quite a story to tell. It seemed that his brother, who was also gay, had contracted AIDS and died, which had caused a great deal of pain, not only for him but for his parents as well. Now with his partner dying he was very concerned about his own health, not so much for his own sake, but for his mother. He wasn't sure that she could go though it a second time.

We talked of faith, death and dying, about relationships and about love. He told me that he had just about given up finding someone to love when two years ago he met Fred. Now Fred was dying, and Fred wasn't Fred anymore because his mind was gone. Roger was a very sensitive man who wasn't sure how he would cope with the disease if and when it hit him. He wouldn't have that special person in his life, and he didn't want to make his mother suffer through it again by going home to be cared for.

A few days later, we went out for dinner at a wonderful Mexican restaurant. This time we talked about our backgrounds, education, interests, and, oh yes, more conversation about our faith, and why we believed as we did. In other words, we shared what our faith meant to us at that time, and how our beliefs had evolved into the peaceful reassurance that the crisis we were sharing had some meaning. Roger and I also shared a love of learning and travel. We had a wonderful time discussing our school experiences and speaking of all the places we had visited.

Roger told me that it was in grade school when he felt different and left out. He had heard the word homosexual, so he looked it up and studied the subject. He was facing himself. He had been active in Sunday School and church, but finally he had to quit, realizing that he wasn't really included in the Kingdom of God (according to the congregation) because of what he was. He was afraid and scared, as only a child could be, thinking that he might be relegated to hell. Finally, after much study and prayer, he realized he was accepted by God just as he was and he found peace.

Those evenings with Roger were a welcome diversion from the hospital and its all-consuming grief.

## Bentley

Meanwhile back home, Tom was dealing with a situation that was both a blessing and a problem.

Tom had always loved animals and his parents had a cat named Bentley, which was his cat when he still lived at home. Connie and Phil were temporarily moving into a residence that did not allow animals, so they called Tom and asked if he would like to have Bentley for awhile. As excited as a child, Tom said, "Yes."

Bentley was used to sleeping on the furniture and having people around all the time. When he arrived, this posed a few problems. He had long white fur, so he left a tell-tale trail wherever he went, and when Tom was dressed for work in his dark suit and tie, Bentley would rub up against his legs, leaving him with fur-trimmed trousers.

The cat was fairly quiet during the day, but at night when the bedroom doors were closed he wandered through the rest of the house meowing at the top of his lungs. I think the love affair between Tommy and his cat was beginning to wane.

## "Is This the Little Boy I Carried?"
### "Sunrise, Sunset"

The day Tim was admitted I had met a young man named David who was part of a very close Jewish family. David had been in Europe with a traveling theatre group when he became ill. This was a dose of harsh reality for this family, as they found out about his homosexuality at the same time they learned about the disease.

David was recovering from pneumocystis and was in the conference room when we came in. The nurses took me down there for coffee while Tim was settled in and hooked up. It was there that David and I met and shared some of the realities of the present situation.

Third floor west was occupied by handsome young men in various stages of many illnesses brought on by AIDS. Tim had been through so much and was so ill that he was in the extreme deterioration stage, while David had just begun on his journey of life with AIDS and still looked healthy and handsome. It was difficult to comprehend that all of these young men would probably be dead within a year.

David's family loved him very much. It was unusual

to see a father as devoted to his gay son as David's father was. He was there most of the day, everyday. His mother was so upset and broken by the situation that she could only be there for short periods of time before being overwhelmed by the enormity of the circumstances. She could never be present when the doctor came for rounds, because she was afraid that he would have only bad news. It is so difficult to assimilate the idea that your handsome, healthy son is homosexual, which dispels the average American dream, and to know he has been handed a death sentence is almost too much to bear in a such short time.

**Ready for his part
in "Bye Bye Birdie"**

## Colorado Springs:
## Pam, Tim, Grandma and Grandpa Foote

**Singing Together**

# TWENTY-NINE

## A Fragile Thread Of Life

### Can't Walk Anymore

One morning Tim looked up at me and said, "Mom, I can't walk anymore." With tears in my eyes, I took his hand and said, "I know Tim, and you know you won't ever walk out of here." He was quiet for awhile and then started a conversation about something else and never spoke to me of walking again.

The next morning it seemed that he had to prove something to himself and asked the nurses to help him out of bed to a chair. They made it to the chair, so Tim sat there while his bed was made. He was then lifted from the chair; Tim took a step and then fell. With assistance from others and with much difficulty the nurses got him back in bed. He never got out of bed again. He could no longer deny the limitations he was suffering because of the disease.

# Closing Down

Tim's digestive and elimination systems were getting worse, and it was becoming impossible for him to eat at all. This presented another major decision for Tim to make. If he wanted to continue nourishment, a Hickman catheter would have to be put into his body through which he could be infused with a high calorie mixture. When in place he would never eat or drink by mouth again.

The Hickman catheter is first inserted with tubing running under the skin to a site where a major vein is penetrated. The vein then carries the tubing directly into the heart, and whatever is infused is immediately metabolized into the body. This kind of catheter minimizes the chance of infection. So this was another philosophical decision for Tim to make. The question was, did he want to starve to death or go for life again and wait for the cancer to kill him by attacking another organ? What a choice, but there were no other alternatives. He decided to allow the force feeding and hang on the fragile thread of life a little longer.

Even though he could not eat and was receiving calories only via the catheter, he began to suffer abdominal pain and would vomit a greenish-brown liquid. A gravity pump was brought in and a tube was pushed down Tim's nostril into his stomach. As the pump was started it began to suck the waste out of Tim's stomach. The tubing was uncomfortable but it was the lesser of two evils because it relieved the cramps and stopped the vomiting.

The purple lesions were spreading and merging as the cancer progressed. His left arm was now one large lesion from the elbow to the wrist, and it had opened up and was constantly weeping so it had to be bandaged every two hours. Some of the smaller lesions were also beginning to open up. Some months before, Letitia told me this would happen, yet I didn't know how bad it would be.

Going home was on Tim's mind. He wanted to die at home with only his loved ones around and in the midst of all the things that had made his and Tom's life together unique and meaningful. When he asked, I said that it would be fine, Tom and I could handle that. However, he would have to choose which pieces of mechanical equipment he would take home and what would be left behind. I didn't think we could manage everything.

The other things he had to consider would be that we would have to have a nurse on duty 24 hours a day and that he would not see Dr. Knight every day. After he pondered the alternatives for awhile, he made the decision to stay in the hospital.

Every day was about the same, I would call the hospital early and ask Tim's nurse what kind of night he had and how he was doing. I would go into the hospital between 10:00 and 10:30 A.M. Some mornings when I came in Vickie would be bathing Tim, and I would help with the lifting and holding.

Tim's arms and legs could no longer be straightened out. It was as though his body was returning to the fetal position. He was very swollen, and his skin was like wax. As I lifted, held or pushed against him, my handprints would remain in his flesh. Vickie asked me how I was able to do the things I did as I was totally involved in his care. But then she answered her own question, saying "I guess

185

mothers do what we have to do."

One day I was a mess when Dr. Knight walked in. He took me into another room and talked to me saying, "Beverly, you are either experiencing a breakdown, or you are very close to it." It was true. The worst part was never knowing when it was going to end. By this time we had been at the hospital for almost a month and we never knew what to expect next. Dr. Knight prescribed some medication for me and gave me the name and phone number of a friend of his, a woman who had lost her son, Chuck, a year before.

**The end is in sight, late summer 1986**

# THIRTY

## Nothing More To Do

### Barbara – A Life Line To Sanity

I contacted Barbara immediately and we made plans for dinner that evening. It is indeed a blessing to be exposed to so many people and to have the opportunity to become friends. She came up to the third floor at the hospital but didn't immediately walk into the room. She waited until she was given Tim's permission; then she came in and remarked about all the flowers and cards, and then she conversed with Tim for a little while before we left for the restaurant.

I rode with her as she knew more about the restaurants in the area. She took me to a pleasant family restaurant. We went in; each of us ordered a glass of wine and began a conversation about her dead son and my dying son.

She said that her son was always an adventurous soul who liked to race motorcycles. She told me about the parties he attended and the circle of friends he had, which

187

included some very famous people. A few years back he had been in an accident and needed to have blood transfusions. It was only the year before, as he was becoming well-known for his racing in Europe, that he became ill and had to come home.

After he was diagnosed he, like so many others, believed he would beat it. For a while he could function normally, but as the disease progressed he had to live somewhere where he could get some help. Barbara was divorced and had a long-term live-in relationship with a fine man whom she loved very much. She felt that it wouldn't be fair to her partner or her son to have him move in with them, so Chuck moved in with his sister. Eventually he went to Sherman Oaks Hospital where he spent the rest of his life.

Chuck could not even consider death as a possibility. He was very fearful as he was forced to realize that he wasn't going to leave the hospital alive. One day Dr. Knight went into his room and spent a great deal of time with him simply talking about life, death and the concept of the transition. Barbara said that whatever Dr. Knight said to him seemed to calm his fears, and he was more peaceful about what was happening to him. He could never talk about it, but was no longer denying it.

Barbara is a professional typist, working at home all morning until early afternoon. At the time Chuck was in the hospital she would go in everyday at 2:00 P.M. and stay with him until around 10:00 at night, or whenever he fell asleep. He died one morning and, as so many of us mothers do, she held him and talked to him. Through her tears she told him how much she loved him and said the final goodbye. Then she sat down outside his room and ate her lunch. There was nothing more to do—he was gone from her.

I told her about Tim, his difficulties and his joys, his wonderful loving relationship with Tom and about my feelings of loss already. Tim was still alive, and yet I knew that in a short time I too would be sitting in his room with his dead body. I would be grieving my loss, but I would know that Tim was totally healed and at peace in a much kinder place, which would give me comfort. Barbara and I said goodbye, promising to keep in contact and to enrich our friendship by meeting and sharing again.

## Back to my Reality

Back at the hospital one morning, Tim requested that the nurse wash his hair. This had to wait until after his bath. Occasionally Tim messed the diapers he now was wearing (there is a great deal of blood now) so the bath had to wait until the diapers were changed. He was also catheterized occasionally to clear his bladder. He wouldn't let them leave it in because it was just another tube, and how he hated that.

The diapers were changed and Vickie and I gave him his bath, but we did not have time to do the shampoo, which done in a bed requires two persons. For this purpose there is a flat, basin-like receptacle with minimal sides on it and a drain on one side. It can be put under the patient's head and water is poured over the hair, always keeping the shallow basin tilted toward the drain side. The patient is then shampooed, and the process is repeated for rinsing. When finished you slide it out from under the patient's head and put his head down on towels. It is a remarkable little invention.

About 1:00 P.M., Roger beckoned to me and asked me to go to lunch with him. It seemed there had been no response from Fred for the last few days. I told him that we had to give Tim a shampoo first and that I wanted to be around when Dr. Knight came as I had some questions. Roger waited around until two o'clock and finally decided to go. Being fairly sure Vickie would be free shortly so we could wash Tim's hair and also believing Dr. Knight would show up soon, I told him I would meet him at the restaurant.

Finally Vickie was available and we got the shampoo out of the way, but there was still no sign of Dr. Knight. Heaven only knew when I would get out of there. Because he left work early, Tom showed up and I went on my way for lunch. (It was now about 3:30 P.M.) I met Roger as he was coming back to the hospital, so I went into the restaurant and sat down alone. A few minutes later Roger returned, and so we had another time of reflection about our lives, the hopes and dreams he and Fred had, and about the reality of the present situation. We talked about the things that were so difficult for us to do: the contact with the mortuaries, the funeral arrangements, and simply letting go of the ones we loved so much, fully realizing that they would never leave the hospital alive and that they would never be with us again. We both had faith that this wasn't the end of life, only the end of life as we know it.

He had other concerns because Fred was quite a wealthy man, and since there is nothing legally binding in any union of two men, even if it is a life-time commitment, he was afraid that Fred's will would be contested by his family and others. He didn't want ugliness and dissension to mar Fred's passing.

It was now approaching the last week of Tim's life. His voice was just a whisper. The ugly purple lesions were spreading to his face. The disease was on an unrelenting attack to devour his whole body. Tim had managed to survive past his birthday, but we knew he would never see Christmas.

A few weeks prior, I had made airline reservations to Denver and would visit Pam and her family at Thanksgiving. I knew I had to get away but didn't want to leave Tim to die while I was gone. I decided I couldn't worry about it and had to take one day at a time.

**We Loved Him Well!**

## Respite: Thanksgiving with Family
### after Tim's passing,

**Missed you this year, Tim.**

# THIRTY-ONE

## "It Is Finished"

### Early Christmas

One beautiful, warm California afternoon Tom showed up with flowers, a Teddy bear dressed in cap, scarf, mittens and with sleigh bells attached, and a gift wrapped in Christmas paper. He was supplying Tim with an early Christmas. I saw love over and over again as Tom gave so unselfishly of himself.

Tim smiled and there were tears in his eyes as he tried to embrace Tommy as Tommy hugged him. Because of the lesions on his face Tim had not been able to shave for several days.

Tom opened his gift for Tim. It was an electric razor that would allow Tommy to shave him without cutting the lesions. Tim thanked him, but he would never use it because he still had a vestige of vanity thinking his beard helped hide the disfiguring blotches on his face. Tommy would be the only one to use the razor, after Tim died.

Tim's condition was deteriorating, and he was rapidly becoming a piece of human wreckage. (I thanked God his mind had been spared.) Although he was suffering the most extreme indignities that could be heaped upon a human being, his fierce sense of pride remained as he tried to maintain a certain level of appearance, awareness and decorum. However, all the time in the hospital and even at the end, Tim's eye problem haunted him. Whenever anyone would come into the room, the first thing he would ask was for his glasses. He was still the little boy who felt unacceptable because of his flaw.

Tim had completed a total life cycle in twenty-seven years. As a baby he had needed total care. He now needed total care. He had grown into a man, independent and free. He had searched out and found love. Soon he would leave his body with all its physical limitations and would know a greater freedom than is possible on this earth. He will find love, also beyond our comprehension ... and he won't have to search it out ... God's love.

## Goodbye

Exactly a week before Thanksgiving on Thursday evening Jeff came up to visit Tim. Jeff would be leaving Friday morning for his home in the Midwest, knowing he would probably never see Tim again. I left the three of them alone, and Jeff was able to say all the things to Tim that he had never been able to express in words before. He reminisced about the good and bad parts of their lives as best friends, told him how much he cared, and what a deep loss Tim's going would be to him. When he said goodbye and left the room he was crying like a baby, unashamedly. Jeff had lost others who were so close, a former lover, a cousin and now his best friend. He was wiped out. (He has since lost another cousin.)

Sunday Chuck and Andy came to see Tim again. They put up a brave front, but when they said goodbye the tears flowed freely, for they were sure this was the final goodbye. The tears were also streaking Tim's face as he knew that all of these wonderful friends who had been with him throughout his life and death struggles would soon be lost to him.

I stayed late that evening. Tom had gone home for much- needed rest, so I sat alone with my son, my dearly beloved son. It was painful to look at this emaciated young man, whom I loved so much. The hospital personnel had installed an overhead rod and handle so he could move and lift himself into a different more comfortable position. There were no comfortable positions.

A few days earlier he had been shown how to use the computerized pump so that he could regulate the amount of morphine to meet his needs. The night nurse, also named Vickie, came in to rebandage his arm and to make sure everything was working right. Tim liked Vickie and could still joke with her in a faint whisper.

After the necessities were taken care of, Tim and I were left alone again. As I sat and held his hand, I prayed that he might die. I stroked his hand and we spoke about little. Tim was completely lucid; he never would slip into a coma. I am sure that Tim still believed that God could completely restore him if He would; however, we both knew that without that miracle, the end of this life was nearing for him. I hugged his tortured and contorted body as much as was possible and told him how much I loved him. He whispered back, "I love you, Mom." I told him I was leaving for the night and that I wouldn't say, "Hang in there," because I knew he would know when it was time to go. I left him in Vickie's capable hands and went home. Goodnight, Tim, I didn't know it was to be goodbye.

Monday morning I called the hospital as I always did and asked to talk to Vickie (the other one), who was Tim's nurse every day now. She said he had had a quiet night and that she had checked on him just a short time before and he was still sleeping. He would be allowed to awaken when he was ready, and then the daily routine would begin. I told her I would be in about 10:30 and would help her with Tim's bath at that time.

I hung up the phone and proceeded to call Dave, for he was waiting for my morning report. As we were talking there was a call-waiting buzz, so I switched it over and it was Dr. Knight. He simply said, "Bev, Tim is gone. He died peacefully in his sleep. He just stopped breathing."

My prayer for my suffering son had finally been answered. There was so little emotion, only numbness. I returned to Dave and told him, "Our son is dead." From the silence at the other end I knew he was trying to sort through his emotions too. It was hard for him to be so far away from Tim when the end finally came. He had no way of being part of his son's death. We will miss Tim so much.

Next I called Tom at work and let him know that Tim was gone. The time he has dreaded has come at last. He will be alone. He would go to the hospital immediately and I would meet him there. By the time Tom got there the nurses had put all of Tim's belongings in plastic bags for us to take home. They had left Tim in his bed as though he were sleeping.

Tom went in and put his arms around Tim and kissed him. He wept as he held Tim's hand and talked to him of many things, private things, words of love and at the end, anger at Tim's leaving him. Forty-five minutes had passed when I arrived and Tom had spent all that time in that hospital room with his beloved Tim.

He went out to give me some time in private with my son, my baby. As I neared the bed, Tim looked so peaceful, at last released from the tubes, machines and needles. I felt his hand and it was warm as was his forehead when I bent down to kiss him. I reached down and touched his feet, and then, as I grasped his hands, the energy of the warmth belied the truth, that Tim no longer lived in this body. He was gone; his soul was with God. He had found his better place at last.

A little later Tom came in. Each of us took one of Tim's hands, we clasped each other's hands and we prayed. We expressed our sorrow and grief in our own loneliness and yet rejoiced in Tim's freedom. After our Amen, Tom started taking things out to the car, bags first, then flowers. As I always do when under stress, I went to the refrigerator. I found the last ice cream bar. Then just like Barbara, I sat there with my dead son and calmly ate my ice cream bar. There was nothing more to do ... he was gone from me.

Tom had finished his task when Steve Kant came in with his companion Max. Max had been released from the hospital a short time ago, but now it seemed he was having some problems again. Steve came in to Tim's room and prayed with us. Then one by one the nurses came in and expressed their sorrow and spoke of their high regard for Tim. It is so difficult for them because whenever one of these young men dies, he takes a part of them with him.

(There should be a special place in heaven for these wonderful people who give so much and are never able to send a patient home to live.)

We stayed a little longer, not wanting to leave until Tim did, pulling down the final curtain on this phase of our lives. The man from the crematory came in, asked us to leave for a few minutes and then came out with Tim enshrouded in a body bag. We rode down the elevator and watched as he took our beloved Tim to the vehicle for his final ride. "Goodbye, Tim! See you later ... someday."

**Love is everywhere in this hospital room**

# THIRTY-TWO

# My Son, J Have Loved You Well

## New Chapter

Barbara was supposed to meet me at the hospital and we were going out for lunch. I was glad she was late, because I wasn't ready to leave yet. It seemed that as long as I was at the hospital, Tim wasn't really dead, and that when I would leave, it would be final. This was my family; all the nurses and doctors were my link with sanity through this time of grief and dying. They had all seen it so many times before.

Finally I went downstairs to wait in the reception area. While there, many people expressed their sympathy. Dr. Knight came and sat in the chair next to me. His grief was apparent as he comforted me. We both knew that we had all fought a good fight and we had nothing to grieve for except our sense of profound loss.

Roger, a hospital volunteer, talked to me expressing how much he envied Tim his family. He could not be honest with his family about himself but always had to be playing a charade. He hated having to do that, but it was a fact of life for him. He shared that his mother was the strong one in the family while his father was very weak and passive. Knowing that some theorize that situation as the cause of homosexuality, there was a time when he hated his father for what he, Roger, was. However, as he became more enlightened, he realized that it probably had no bearing on his sexuality and then could make peace with himself and his parents.

While in the lobby, Carl, a former patient who had known Tim and Tom from their public speaking days, came in. He looked hale and hearty and was in to get some prescriptions filled. He had been in the hospital some time back, had overcome pneumocystis pneumonia, and was now feeling great. He had the beginnings of Kaposi Sarcoma but hoped he could keep it under control. Carl expressed his sorrow over Tim's death but yet rejoiced with me in the fact that Tim was finally free.

Barbara didn't show up so I went over to the Lamplighter restaurant for the last time. I ordered a glass of wine and as I waited for my meal, reflected on the past few weeks and wondered where God was.

Now I could leave California for the Thanksgiving holiday without fear or worry. The memorial service for Tim would not be held until December 7 because so many of his friends were gone for the Thanksgiving weekend, so as I packed my suitcase the knowledge that I would be gone only a little while comforted me. I wasn't ready to let go of everything that reminded me of Tim just yet.

As I said goodbye to Tom it was with concern about leaving him alone at this time. Yet he needed some time alone to sort out his feelings and grieve the loss of his beloved Tim.

During the flight there was much time to think and question. Would it have been better for Tim to have come home to die? He would have been surrounded by the things that made his and Tom's life together meaningful. He would have had only the ones who loved him around. Tom and I would have been there when he died. That thought bothered me. Why weren't we there? Why did he die alone? We had spent so much time at the hospital, why did the end come when neither of us was there? Then I thought, if it is true that many terminally ill people choose the moment to die, I had to believe it was Tim's choice. He must have thought it would have been extremely hard on Tom and me, so he chose a private time with no one around to leave this earthly dimension.

The holiday at Pam's and Doug's home was wonderful. My grandchildren, Sean and Colleen, supplied welcome diversion as did grandson Joshua and his parents, Mike and Sherri. Dave arrived from Lindsborg and my mother flew in from Minnesota, and as I contemplated my family, I realized that there is a continuum of love of which Tim is a part. No, he would never be completely gone because he lives with each of us. My family and my faith is my refuge.

The day came when it was time to leave Denver to go home for a few days. Lindsborg is a very small town, and people didn't know how to approach Dave and me, or what to say. I found that some avoided us, some hugged us, and some cried with us. The big issue of what to say about Tim's death didn't have to be dealt with immediately. I would wait until after his memorial service to decide what to say. After all, AIDS is not an acceptable disease to die of.

**Celebrating:
Tim's Freedom**

**Goodbye, Tim — We'll see you soon**

# THIRTY-THREE

# Celebration Of Tim's Life

### In Memory

Dave and I were to return to Los Angeles, Thursday, December 4th. There was such a hassle with the flight that I found myself telling the ticket agent, through my tears, that we were going to Los Angeles for our son's funeral and had to get on a certain flight. My anguish made an impression as everything was straightened out shortly. However, the flight was still very late and we didn't arrive at LAX until 1:00 A.M. Friday. We took the shuttle to Tommy's house and got a few hours sleep.

In the morning, Dave went to a business meeting and I picked out the flowers for the service. I chose a beautiful arrangement but wanted something more, something that would last. I wandered around the florist shop and picked out a fig tree as a living memorial for Tom to keep.

Pam and Mike arrived Saturday. They were also going to spend the night at Tom's house. Tommy stayed with

Jeff so there would be room for everyone. That afternoon Mike had to do a little shopping, so he and Dave left the house while Pam and I sorted through Tim's clothing. Tom couldn't wear anything of Tim's, so we took what Dave and Doug could use. Just another one of those difficult things to get through.

In his closet hung the gray three-piece suit. The suit in which he graduated from high school and interviewed for his first job. The suit he took with him the first time he went to California. The suit he was wearing when he served as pall bearer at his grandmother Barbo's funeral. The suit he looked so handsome in. It was hard to say, "Give it away."

Our family went to dinner that night, just to enjoy each other as we had so many times before the children left home. But now one of our members was missing. We spoke of the past and some of the good times. It was good to be together again.

Sunday morning came, the day we would gather to remember and pay tribute to Tim—son, brother, companion and friend. When we arrived at the mortuary we were warmly greeted by Chester, whom I introduced to everyone. He was so extremely caring and made us very comfortable being there.

The room where the service was to be held was light and airy, which gave a feeling of cheerfulness, not heaviness. It was perfect for the service, which was not to be a funeral but a celebration of Tim's life, and now his freedom.

I gave Chester the tapes with the music for the service

and then walked to the front of the room. There, on a small table, was the bronze box containing Tim's remains. Light blue satin was draped over the box. On either side of the box I placed a picture of Tim, one informal in a flannel shirt, flashing a big smile and the other, formal, more serious, wearing the gray three-piece suit. Flowers were lovingly placed on the table and on the floor around it. To one side stood the living fig tree.

There were not many at the service. Our family, Tom's family, those who were Tim's and Tom's best friends, Tim's manager from Pacific Telesis and Barbara. Not many in numbers, yet Tim had touched many lives, and the visits, prayers and acts of kindness shown throughout Tim's struggle would be ever gratifying to us.

As the service began, many in the congregation were crying softly. I shed no tears at this time. There had been many tears the past year and a half, and there would be more to come. I felt a great peace knowing Tim was in the hands of God.

### CELEBRATION OF LIFE – MEMORIAL SERVICE

**Timothy Alan Barbo** (1959 – 1986)

*Sunday, December 7, 1986 at 11:00 A.M.*

*Service conducted by Steve Kant included:*

#### Prayer and Meditation:

Steve spoke of all his conversations with Tim over the past months as they shared from the deepest recesses of their hearts. They had discussed everything from the world situation to the circumstances of their individual lives. They spoke of their loving relationships with Max and Tom. Much of the time they pondered spiritual things—love, God, what this life on earth really meant and what it would mean to die.

As he remembered Tim's love of God, Steve said that he regarded him as a teacher of love, and by observing Tim's struggle with the disease, he considered Tim's life as the ultimate expression of courage. He knew that everyone in the service would remember Tim in his or her individual way, as all of our hearts had been touched by him. As we had all shared with Tim in the physical realm, we would now share in remembrance and love from that special place within our hearts where Tim lived and would always be real to us.

Steve read a portion from an ancient Eastern text which referred to life as ever changing but eternal. He then read from and expanded on John 14, where Christ promises that where He is, we may be also; and from 2 Corinthians: 12:7-10 as the apostle Paul tells about his thorn in the flesh, which he prayed would be removed. Christ's answer was, "My grace is sufficient for you, for my power is made perfect in weakness."

Many times in the past few months of Tim's life Steve questioned why Tim still lived. Yet, as time went on he became more aware of the in-dwelling spirit of Christ, giving Tim peace and freeing him from fear and doubt. Why was he still alive? Perhaps to give everyone the opportunity to complete their relationship with him, whatever it was.

*Remembrances of Tim
by some of those who loved him:*

Dear Tim,                                October 9, 1986

I won't ask how you're doing because I assume it's not too good. I know it's really tough for you physically and mentally, and you probably wake up wondering why you were born having to suffer so much agony. Well I can't answer that question, but I do know that you are, and have been, a tremendous inspiration to me personally. I hope that the courage and tenacity that you possess will become part of me. I'm continually amazed by your refusal to give up and quit when you probably have wanted to a thousand times. I want to let you know that I have the greatest respect and admiration for you. It is an honor and a privilege knowing you, and I have benefited by your existence and struggle.

I know Carol and I believe my folks think the same way. The reason I wrote this letter was that I was feeling down about a couple of things (minor things) and I needed a shot of courage and strength. I got it from you. I just wanted to say Thanks.

Roger (Tom's brother)

Tim,                                    November 7, 1986

It is difficult for me to tell you all of the emotions inside me now. There is confusion, asking "why does it have to be you?" There is guilt, never being able to tell you how much I love and miss you.

There is love, holding the thoughts of you and the

207

wonderful visit of the past summer in my heart and mind. There is pain, knowing that even though we've never been close I'm losing the only brother I've ever had. The bond of brotherhood, no matter how far stretched, can never be severed.

I still find it hard to accept the fact that you will be taken from us in what appears to be a short time.

I'm truly sorry that my son has not gotten the opportunity to know his Uncle Tim. I know my uncles were always very special people, and no doubt Joshua will feel the same way about you and Kevin and Tom. I love you very much.

Mike

December 7, 1986

Tim brought a new understanding of Love:
> Love that brings us out of our self-imposed
>     boxes
> Love that confronts
> Love that teaches
> Love that accepts
> Love that reaches through barriers and defenses
> Love that is unconditional.

Tim was loved:
> Family and friends loved him through these
>     years
> Family and friends loved him through his illness
> Family and friends gave unselfishly out of their
>     love
> I am so proud of you all.

Life goes on because:
>    we have learned patience
>    we have learned endurance
>    we have learned kindness
>    we have learned to hope
>    we have an eternal future.

These things show that Christ was alive in my dear brother, giving him a purpose for life. Let's rejoice in the lives he touched and encouraged, let's rejoice that he is totally healed and at peace.

Let's take the things we've learned to help build each other up, to help others see past their prejudices and fears, and most importantly remember how love is continued through each of us that knew and loved Tim. Then this will not be in vain and God will be glorified.

I loved you Tim. Thanks family for allowing yourselves to grow in love. Thanks to each of you his special friends – you've taught me a lot.

Pam

Dear Tim,                                  December 7, 1986

Well Tim, although the race of life wasn't as long for you as it is for some of us and although it was very strenuous and difficult at the end, you finished it well. We loved you so very much and will miss you, but there is rejoicing in our hearts because we know you are in a much better place.

As you walk into heaven, we can imagine the welcome you must be getting because of all the lives you touched on this old earth.

Dad and I have fond memories of your growing years—all the times we rejoiced with you in your achievements and hurt with you during the painful times. We remember the piano recitals, your playing cello in the string quartet, being part of the Madrigal singers, choirs, church musical groups and drama. Your good grades (also your vocal disagreement with some teachers).

We remember the time you and Ross were taken to the police station for playing army and using firecrackers—we never saw two more terrified young men. We remember your astronaut period of life and Doug's help in building a real spaceship in the backyard.

We had so many good times on all our trips and at our crazy family gatherings. We know your teen years were not always happy for you, but you taught us so much. Dad and I had to climb out of our narrow little boxes and deal with life as it really is, not how we want it to be. We struggled together, Tim, but in this struggle Dad and I learned more about acceptance and unconditional love than we could have any other way.

Your friends are so very special and we have learned to love and appreciate them so much. Pam and Mike got married and added Doug and Sherri to our family. When God put you and Tommy together it was as if he gave us another son. Tommy is truly part of our family and always will be.

Tom has told me of so many of the good times you had together. Those trips you took were very special—Palm Springs, Vegas, Palm Springs, Hawaii, Palm Springs. You taught each other so much and loved each other so much. Your discipline in money matters was a plus in your relationship. Tom's gentleness taught you to be a more gentle person while you helped him to be more assertive.

The great times the both of you had—special dinners at special places, red gladiolas for birthdays and anniversaries, those fun rides in "Miss Parklane," great parties, enjoying the sun and surf together and so much more.

I remember the trip back for my graduation and although you looked so healthy I sensed something was wrong and when you told me, we knew you had some hard times ahead—always hoping and praying that with your strength of body, mind and spirit you would beat it.

Just a year ago was my first "Care for Tim Trip" to LA and I found you so ill. Christmas with Tom's parents was so special— they are exceptional people—and by the time I left LA you were so much better.

You and Tom coming to Minnesota last May to visit grandma, aunts, uncles, cousins, nieces and nephews was a tribute to your faith in your family's love. The love was there. The effort you and Tom put forth to visit his family in Oregon was exceptional. What a wonderful time you had with wonderful people.

Love, that's what it is all about—not just words but reaching out to touch and hold each other in joy and sorrow.

We will never forget your tenacity when you first entered the hospital, beating all odds, and how much you more or less directed your care through the whole time. These last weeks and months have been very difficult, but you gave it your best shot. I thank God that Dad, Pam and Mike all had a time with you. I am so happy that I was allowed to be such an integral part of your life and part of your transition.

Dad and I thank God for the prayer of so many and especially the little children praying for their Uncle Tim.

Most of all Dad and I thank God for you, Tim. You changed our lives and hopefully made us kinder, more loving people. We will miss you.

Well, say "hi" to everyone there—give those we love an big hug and throw Ginger an extra bone (if dogs have to eat there).

We love you and will see you soon.

Love, Mom

## THE LOAN

*I'll lend you for a little time,*
*a child of mine, God said;*
*For you to love the while he lives,*
*and mourn for when he's dead.*

*It may be six or seven years,*
*or twenty-two or three*
*But will you, 'till I call him back,*
*take care of him for Me?*

*He'll bring his charms to gladden you,*
*and shall his stay be brief*
*You'll have his lovely memories*
*as solace for your grief.*

*I cannot promise he will stay*
*since all from earth return,*
*But there are lessons taught down there,*
*I want this child to learn.*

*I've looked in the wild world over,*
*in my search for teachers true,*
*And from the throngs that crowd life's lanes,*
*I have selected you.*

*How will you give him all your love,*
*Not think the labor vain,*
*Nor hate me when I come*
*to take him back again?*

*I fancied that I heard them say:*
*"Dear Lord, Thy will be done!"*
*For all the joy Thy child shall bring,*
*the risk of grief we'll run.*

*We'll shelter him with tenderness,*
*we'll love him while we may,*
*And for the happiness we've known,*
*forever grateful stay.*

*But shall the angels call him*
*much sooner than we've planned,*
*We'll brave the bitter grief that comes,*
*and try to understand.*

## AUTHOR UNKNOWN

Tom's love and devotion for Tim had been very apparent as he unselfishly cared for Tim through the critical period of life and death. Among the momentos Tom treasured was a card Tim had written to him for one of their anniversaries.

*Love —*

*I have learned about love from you — and yet have so much more still to gain. Teach me, Tom, in your ways of freedom, honesty and peace. Help me to open up to all the wonderful love that is being offered. The Love of Christ is radiating from you.*

*I will always Love You.*

Tim

*P.S. — While arranging the flowers the two roses went in together last. No matter how I tried to arrange them differently, the roses clung together — just like you and I.*

Music to affirm our faith in Christ's promise found in John 14:1-3:

*"Let not your hearts be troubled; ye believe in God, believe also in me. In my Father's house are many mansions; if it were not so, I would have told you. I will come again and receive you unto myself, that where I am, there ye may be also."*

## "It Is Well With My Soul"

## "It Is Finished"

We are grateful for the dimension Tim added to our lives. We now release our loved one into God's abiding light, knowing all is well with him. We in our humanness, feeling loss, will gratefully accept God's comfort.

When the Barbo family sang together, Tim had a solo

in **"Let's Go Fly a Kite"** from **"Mary Poppins,"** so to lift our spirits let us listen to:

Music to celebrate Tim's freedom –

## **"Let's Go Fly A Kite"**

and release the balloons

After the service everyone went back to Tom's house for a time of refreshment and fellowship. Jeff had been in charge of the refreshments. He had ordered some food, and many of their friends brought their special dishes. We offered a toast to Tim's freedom and to the fact that we would be seeing him again someday—to the promise of a new and better life.

Mike, the attendant who had been with Tim at the end of his home stay, stopped in to express his condolences. He had just gotten off his shift from working with another AIDS patient. He stayed and got acquainted with everyone. Pam made quite an impression on him; as he told Tom, "She's really nice, for a girl." Barbara and I had a wonderful conversation. Pam and Mike were enjoying themselves immensely and Dave was having a business discussion with Brian. Connie and Phil, as well as Tom's brother, seemed to fit right in. Bentley was complaining loudly because he was shut in the bedroom. As they were leaving I hugged Connie and said, "I hope and pray you don't have to go through this." It is better that we don't know what is ahead.

Tommy told me later, that he didn't know what to expect as he had never been to a funeral service before. He realized that this celebration service was good and just what he had needed to put a final ending to that chapter of his life. Of course the grief and loneliness would be there, but perhaps it wouldn't be overwhelming.

Dave and I took Pam and Mike to the airport. On the way they both spoke with such high regard for Tim's and Tom's friends. Mike said, "Mom, I have a whole new perspective on Tim's situation. Everyone should have as good friends as Tim had, I should have such good friends."

Monday morning I went to the hospital to give them a memorial folder. Amy thanked me for it and said, "We appreciate the picture taken when he was well, we only see them when they are very sick."

I walked over to Dr. Knight's office to give him a memorial folder. Jeannine ushered me in; both she and Dr. Knight gave me a hug. They were very appreciative of the remembrance of Tim and we spoke a while remembering him.

Before I left the office, I requested to have my blood tested. I felt that as long as I had lived with Tim and Tom for six months out of the last year and that I had taken very personal care of Tim, that my blood should be tested. I didn't want people to be afraid of me. Dr. Knight chuckled a little and reassured me that I had nothing to worry about, but he agreed to do it for me. Jeannine came in and drew my blood. Later the results proved negative.

That evening, Dave and I went out for dinner with Tom and Jeff. This is the end of my California sojourn, and tomorrow Dave and I will leave this place. "Please God, spare Tom!" I pray there will be no second time around.

# THIRTY-FOUR

# A Time For Everything Under Heaven

## Now

Tim's story is unique, yet as each of us has a personal story, we find we are part of a diverse humanity. There was much hurt and pain in Tim's life that most people, even family, were not aware of, because I was the only one he really confided in as he was growing up. I am sure that some who knew Tim were not aware of his constant struggle and therefore would not agree with this interpretation. However, this was Tim's truth and reality as he and I perceived it.

There were many good and happy times in Tim's life that have not been recorded, such as parties for every birthday, Christmas gatherings, the special programs in school and church, the many family trips we took over the years, the wonderful performance he gave in his first high school drama and the warm camaraderie expressed by

217

everyone in the troupe, good times as a family performing as the Barbo Family Quartet, Quintette or Sextette, (depending on how many were present) and much, much more.

Later in life after he and Tom had found each other, he experienced what it was like to belong and be loved. They had disagreements and arguments as any two people living together do, but there was always the coming together in a sense of family.

Many gay people grow up without the hassle and trauma Tim experienced. Tom is one of these. In spite of the fact that he knew he was different, he functioned well in the straight community until he found a time and a place as well as people he could trust to be open with about who he was.

Although background experiences were different, family and spiritual values were very similar. In the search for that special person in their lives, God allowed Tom and Tim to find each other, and as the loving exchange grew, the relationship matured into a complementary completeness.

Perhaps within the context of God's love and this community of the gentle people, it is time we looked positively upon the committed lifetime relationship, thereby validating a permanent arrangement and minimizing the promiscuity problem.

This comes from my heart, the mother of one of the gentle people who because he didn't fit the norm, was severely wounded by society, sought love (or what he thought was love) where he could, and was then mortally wounded because of that search. Everyone has to belong somewhere and be loved by someone if life is to have any meaning.

As parents of a homosexual, Dave and I felt the usual shame and humiliation. We felt guilt ... "What did we do wrong?" At the beginning of this journey we believed it had to be our fault ... or Tim's fault ... Finally after trying to apply band- aids to Tim's life and our own, we realized that our only responsibility was in how we reacted to Tim as a creation of God with all of his inherited imperfections. It was indeed a call to accept and love. We failed the call to accept many times, but never the call to love.

How about our reputation, Dave's and mine? Are we worried about what others think? No more!!! What a relief!! What freedom! We know who we are in the Lord with all of our weaknesses and warts ... accepted. Tim was a unique creation of God ... also accepted. As long as we are secure in God, what other people think of us is of little importance from the perspective of eternity.

There are many books written, programs produced and sermons preached by religious people who in their good intentions tell the gay person how to change. The basic premise always is, "You are under God's condemnation, and mine, until you change and become acceptable." There is so much said by so many about something that they know so little.

I have read the books, watched the programs and listened to the sermons. After living the reality of how things are, I have to quit all of that foolishness and get back to the basics—God—and everything in His good time.

219

Before I could come to this realization I had to come to a time in my life where my strength was gone. There was nothing left of me with which to struggle. I said to God, "I am no longer responsible; you are. Satan, you can leave; I will carry no more guilt nor will I heap guilt on anyone else." Tim is gone, but there are so many others in need. I have been forced to trust God with my son and I know God is sufficient for everyone in need if we let Him be. Are we treating others as Christ would?

As I sat in church today, watching the children as they struggled to get lined up just right, to find their proper place, and then listened as they sang their praise to God, I thought back to the time when my children stood in front of the congregation. I could still see that little blond boy with the horn-rimmed glasses singing as though his heart would burst with love.

I remembered when, with sure and steady steps, he walked into the baptismal waters signifying his death and resurrection with Jesus Christ ... and I wept.

Tim has been released. As people call for mandatory testing and speak of quarantine, I am glad he didn't live to see that ... to be dehumanized, labeled and wounded again. He is free indeed. Free of the fear of being found out, free of the cruelty and rejection of others, free of the fear of not being acceptable to God.

Dear Tim, the path in this journey of life gave us mountains to climb over, forests to find our way through, crevices to fall into and many obstacles to trip over. Stones were thrown that wounded us, but we made it through, family intact plus Tom. You just happened to make it to the final destination before the rest of us. We could have done no more. We loved and received love.

I truly believe that what we have had faith in for so long is true. I know that where you are it is wonderful and that you have indeed found your better place … Home at last.

Amen – So Be It

Love,

Mom

**Family, May 28, 1985**

# END NOTES

Scripture references in this book are from the **"Revised Standard Version."** Copyright 1962 by "The World Publishing Company," Cleveland, Ohio. Usage permission requested.

[1] Freud, Sigmund. "The Psychogenesis of a Case of Homosexuality in a Women," **Collected Papers**, vol 2 (New York: Basic Books, 1959), pp. 206-7.

[2] Boyd, Malcolm. "Am I Running With You, God?" Mary Yost Associates, New York, N.Y. Usage permission requested.

[3] McNaught, Brian. "On Being Gay." 1986. TRB Productions, P. O. Box 2361, Boston, MS 02109.